FOUR ALPHAS, FOUR BABIES

PREGNANT WITH FOUR ALPHAS' BABIES

BOOK SIX

BELLA MOONDRAGON
OLIVIA BHELLE KILDARE

ROGUE WOLF
PUBLISHING

For our friends at Rogue Wolf Publishing

CONTENTS

CHAPTER 1: FRIEND OR ENEMY?

Rose

Alpha Kane rushes off, leaving me alone with just the woman who was in here earlier. She is staring at me with a puzzled look on her face, and I want to tell her she should go help with the invasion, but I am under the impression that she has been assigned to guard me.

At least it's her and not one of those other two guys. They were both so stupid, I'd probably be able to trick them into leaving me alone long enough to get out of here without them being able to catch me, but at the same time, they were creepy, and I don't trust them not to do something stupid or weird.

"So…" she finally says, folding her arms under her chest. Her blunt haircut makes her look older than she is, I think. Her skin is smooth and clear. She's actually pretty, when she's not glaring at me like she wants to kill me. "I guess that bit about not remembering shit was a bunch of lies then?"

I shrug. "Desperate times call for desperate measures."

"How did you think that was going to help exactly?" she asks me, and she's giving me the same look that she gave those two men when they'd say something stupid.

"Well, my theory was that maybe if I didn't remember who I was, no one would think that I was a threat," I tell her. "They would think I was just some helpless pregnant woman and leave me the hell alone." I hope that makes sense to her. "It's not like I had a lot of time to think of a strategy. I had to do something. You heard Kane's plan for me and my children, right?"

She shrugs. "Serves you right. Rich Alpha's daughter bitch with four lovers."

My eyes widen. "Uhm, clearly, you don't know anything about me."

She scoffs, a laugh escaping her lips. "Which part of what I said was wrong exactly? Your father is an Alpha, which automatically makes you rich, and those four Alphas knocked you up, so whether they love you or not, they're still your lovers, right?"

I narrow my gaze at her. "First of all, my father is a horrible Alpha. He misappropriated a whole bunch of funds, and we are far from rich. Kane and Stephen attacked him, so I have no idea what's left of my pack, but I'm sure my people are struggling right now."

She is staring at me intently, but she doesn't roll her eyes or accuse me of lying.

So I continue. "Then, you should know that I have had anything but a glamorous life up until the time that I came to the castle, and quite frankly afterward. Back in my home pack, because my parents had spent so much money they weren't supposed to, I had to take a job in a neighboring pack at the sewage treatment plant. I had to shovel shit for a living. That was just one of the jobs I've had in my life, so coming to Castle Black Rock to become a Breeder wasn't exactly my choice. I just did what my parents told me to do."

Her eyes stay on me for a long time, like she's not sure what to say to me. I think she believes me, though. Eventually, she says, "You're not the woman I thought you were. Kane says you're a spoiled, rich brat, something like Barbara, I guess, and if we kill you, the world will be a better place. He says that your babies will be the equivalent of demon babies, and we may as well kill them, too. He says the Alphas are a bunch of conceited assholes who want to rule the world."

"It sounds to me like Kane is the one who needs to either be killed or put in his place," I say with a shrug. "He's not being honest with any of you, and he's making you do things you don't want to do just because he's your Alpha and he can boss you around."

She seems like a smart woman. She continues to think about what I'm saying to her, chewing on her thumbnail now.

"Listen, you have to know that Kane can't possibly defeat all four of the Alphas and their armies, right?" I ask her.

"Well, he has help. Alpha Stephen, for one, is helping him. There are others, too."

I shake my head. "No one is going to be able to beat the four Alphas. They are the strongest, most powerful Alphas in the kingdom. That's why King Gene chose them to be the ones to participate in this contest to begin with. So... Alpha Kane will lose, and when he does, the people who fight on his side are going to have to pay for what they've done. Do you want to be the person who was responsible for watching me when I died?"

She swallows hard but doesn't speak.

"What's your name?" I ask her, using a gentle voice.

"What difference does it make?" she asks, defensively. "Are you trying to get me in trouble?"

I smile and shake my head. "No. Just curious. You know my name. I wanted to know yours."

She hesitates a bit longer before she says, "Diana."

"Hi, Diana," I say, thinking I might actually be friends with her under different circumstances.

"Hi," she says, but she doesn't seem very enthusiastic. In fact, since I mentioned to her that she'd be in big trouble when this is all over, she looks very nervous.

"I think, though, you have a good opportunity to change the tides here, you know? If you can help me, then, when this is all over, I'll be able to tell the Alphas that you were a friend to me, that they owe you, and when one of them is the new king, they can reward you for your help."

I hold my breath, watching her, hoping she's willing to help me because I don't think I can do this on my own.

It takes a long while, but eventually, she nods and says, "Fine. I'll do it."

A smile spreads across my face. "Thank you," I say.

"It won't be easy, though. You're carrying four pups, and there are guards everywhere. It's not like I can dress you up like a soldier."

"Are there any secret passages or anything?" I ask her.

She shakes her head. "No. But I do have a plan. Do you trust me?"

I inhale sharply and then let it out really slowly. "Do I have a choice?"

A smile spreads across her face and she replies, "No, you don't. Come with me."

Reluctantly, I push up off of the bed and get to my feet, unsteady from all of the drugs. I've got to make this work, one way or another.

CHAPTER 2: PART OF BEING ON THE TEAM

Eli

It would be faster to heal if I stayed in wolf form, but the tiny seats in these utility vehicles aren't exactly built for four legs. Since my hand is still injured, I'm stuck riding shotgun while Kelly drives. And I wish she'd go faster.

She'd insisted that I eat, but I didn't want to waste time, so I inhaled about half a sandwich before I finally convinced her to leave, so now I'm finishing up the rest of it one-handedly while we speed through the forest. Luckily there's a rough path here, so the vehicles are making good time, although in wolf form we may be able to run faster—but again, there's my injured hand, so I'd probably trudge along like a snail.

While I'm in a generally useless state, I have time to think. There's an ache deep in my gut whenever I think of Rose being kidnapped, and that's making it more difficult to finish the sandwich. Though I could easily ask Kelly what happened at the castle, I really don't think I want to hear the details. I know Rose would never let anyone take her alive, so imagining what someone had done to drag her out of there is just… unthinkable.

The result of whatever happened is that Rose is missing, and she's probably been kidnapped by Kane's people, which means she's in the hands of Kane right now. At that thought, I'm completely done with my sandwich, but I force myself to down some water because I'm going to need the hydration to heal up and fight that evil bastard. Out of all the Alphas, he's the lowest because he's willing to kill anyone he needs to just to have as much power as he can grab. Well, maybe Rose's father is the lowest after what he's done to her throughout her life.

But Kane… he's terrifying, which means whoever he has guarding Rose will never go against his commands. I never want to harm innocent wolves, but I'll have no choice if they stand in between me and Rose.

I look over at Kelly, who is really focused on driving, so I decide not to bother her. She probably doesn't know where our armies are anyway. 'Reece,' I say in the mind-link.

'Eli? Are you okay?'

'I'm fine,' I tell him. 'What's the situation?'

'We have our main forces headed to Kane,' he says. 'But the other Alphas and I are going after Stephen.'

'What?! Why?'

'Barbara said that Stephen took her,' he says.

'And you believe her?' That knot in my stomach has turned into pure anger, and it's welling up in my chest.

'No,' he says. 'But if it's true, then we'll waste time with Kane while Rose and the pups are still in danger. It's pretty much on the way to Kane's anyway, so we're taking the chance. If she's not in Stephen's castle, then we can get to Kane fairly quickly.'

I take a deep breath. It's a gamble, but he's right. I know Barbara is working with Kane and would do anything to help him. But on the other hand, Barbara is all about Barbara, so if it's in her best interest to help us—which it is since we'll be the ones ruling the kingdom—then she's just as likely to sell Kane out without hesitating. If we ignore her, then Stephen could be hurting Rose right now. We just can't take the chance. But with three Alphas heading toward Stephen, my place is with the troops going after Kane.

'I'm headed to Kane,' I tell him.

'You're in no shape for that,' says Mark. Apparently, Reece had brought the other Alphas into the mind-link conversation.

'I'm fine,' I say. 'Kelly brought herbs from the healers and they're working fine. Nothing is going to keep me away from Rose. We need an Alpha overseeing the Kane attack.'

There's silence, so I know everyone understands that there's no sense in trying to talk me out of it. We all feel the same way about Rose, and we just need to rescue her as soon as we can.

'We'll get her,' Tristan says, and then we disengage the mind-link. We all have troops to command and no time to waste chatting about it.

And that's exactly what I do, contacting my warriors to get their position so we meet up with them before they reach Kane's fortress. I'm so pissed about Cora, and I pray to the Moon Goddess that she didn't bring any of my trusted warriors over to her side, whatever her side is. I'll have to worry about that later.

The landscape flies by at a dizzying pace, with specks of green blending into the deep browns of tree trunks as the smell of pine and cedar fills the air. I close my eyes, needing a moment to regroup inside my head before we meet up with our troops. Images of Rose flow through my mind—lingering on one picture of her smiling face gazing at me drearily as we wake up from a night of lovemaking. The pain of missing her is biting, but I can't help smiling at her beautiful face as the memory of her scent dances in my mind.

I feel a sudden, violent jerk and open my eyes to see the bushes and trees still moving by quickly, but I'm no longer in the utility vehicle—my body is flying forward. I shift mid-air and jump down with too much forward momentum, landing violently on my injured front paw and letting out an ear-piercing howl as I roll on the ground, the pine needles mixing with the blood on my fur until I finally come to a stop at a giant tree.

Adam

'Take one for the team,' I say in my mind, 'The Alphas need you.' I've been repeating my little mantra for the past hour, but I don't think I've convinced myself that sitting here listening to Barbara and Gene bicker about—clothes?—is somehow going to win the war on Kane and get Rose back. But since it's all my fault that she's gone, I sigh.

I can't believe I didn't guard that damn secret passage door.

"I am to be the Luna Queen!" Barbara hollers. "How can I be seen in these worthless rags? They're hardly worth burning in the castle furnace for heat!" She seems to have perfected the art of bellowing almost as effectively as Gene has.

"These are made of the finest fucking silk!" screams Gene. No, he's still the champion at bellowing.

"I don't give a fuck what they're made of," she says. "I'm not going to be caught dead in these drab colors and unflattering styles. I'll need the royal seamstress to start from scratch."

They rattle on for several more minutes, and I close my eyes, just to give myself a few milliseconds of peace.

"Adam!"

I jump in my seat and open my eyes to see Gene's face no more than twelve inches away from my own. It's horrifying.

"Y—Your Majesty," I say.

There's silence as he stares at me without speaking, and I can see that he's even drooling a little.

"You're to escort Luna Barbara to the seamstress to measure her for new outfits!" He finally backs away from me, and I'm guessing it's so that I can get up and take Barbara where he's ordered me to. I'm torn as to whether this is a good thing or not, but I guess going from dealing with two of them to just one is a win. Yes, I'll call it a win.

"Yes, Your Majesty," I say as I stand up, give Gene a half-assed sign of respect and heading toward the door.

He's already pouring a drink at his private bar when I close the door behind Barbara and me. I need a drink myself right now.

"Well?!"

Now Barbara's face is in front of me, and while she has somewhat attractive features, she has a nasty habit of contorting them into horrifying configurations that make her look like a witch. I quickly dodge her and wish I had some bleach to clean that awful image out of my mind, and we both head toward the sewing room to find the seamstress.

She keeps talking while we walk, babbling on about nothing and clanking her heels on the floor. I don't know how she walks in those huge heels. They seem to defy gravity. To tune her out, I escape into my own head for a while... Shelby, yes, she'll do it for me. She's so hot, and I remember how I snuck up behind her in the shower a few days ago and grabbed her gorgeous ass from behind. She was mad at first, but then I reached my fingers around and massaged her nipples until they were all perky and delicious, then I turned her around and tasted them. They were fabulous.

I'm almost at the sewing room door now, so I come out of my thoughts and realize that I've successfully tuned out Barbara. I don't hear her babbling—or her heel clacking, come to think of it—anymore. I turn around and face a blank hallway.

Fuck. I had one job, and I blew it once again.

CHAPTER 3: GET HELP

ROSE

"Where are we going?" I ask Diana as she leads me out of the room where Kane had intended for me to stay toward the sound of troops shouting and running outside. I think they must be preparing to shift in order to go fight against the Alphas, and I don't want to go that way. It seems dangerous to me.

"We're going to Alpha Kane's office," she tells me.

I stop in my tracks. 'What? Why?" That sounds like an even worse idea than where I'd thought we were going, toward the sound of fighting troops.

"Well, we need a phone," she explains, "and in order to get one, we'll have to go to his office. It's the only phone in the entire castle."

I'm still confused. "But won't he know we're in there?" I ask her.

She shakes her head. "He only spends time in his bedroom banging all of his maids or in the war room shouting orders at his commanders. Other than that, he's usually out on the battlefield. He doesn't spend a whole lot of time in his office."

"What about other people?" I ask, still not walking toward her. "Doesn't he have a secretary or his Beta or something? Someone who would be in or around his office?"

She lets out a loud sigh. "No! I'm telling you, the office is the best place for us to go right now. He'll never look there. It's probably more dangerous for you to be out of your room because he's more likely to go in there and want to harass you than he is to go into his office. But it sounds like your boyfriends are keeping him busy right now, so as long as we hurry, we should be good." She beckons for me to come, and I start walking again, struggling to keep up with my four babies in tow, but I still don't think this is the best idea anyone has ever had.

"Why can't I use the mind-link?" I ask her as I walk along. I've been trying to reach Tristan, Mark, Reece, or even Eli ever since I woke up and discovered where I was, but it hasn't done any good.

"Alpha Kane's got it all clogged up," she says, waving her hand dismissively.

I am confused. "What do you mean all clogged up?" I've never heard of anything like that before.

"Yeah, so he is an Alpha, right? He can keep prisoners from being able to reach their pack mates, family members, even other Alphas. It's a skill a lot of the Alphas have. I bet yours can do it, too."

My mouth drops open, and I stare dumbfounded. I've never heard of anything like that before. "Well... I still don't know how a phone is going to work. It's not like I can just call the Alphas while they're on the battlefield. And even if I do call them, what should I tell them? 'Hi, I'm being held hostage by Kane.' They likely already know that."

She turns the corner quickly without peeking around first, and it makes me nervous to follow her, but she doesn't wait for me, so I have to rush around to catch up with her.

"We can call your parents," she says. "I know you said they were awful to you, but maybe they can get word to the Alphas of where you are. I heard Kane say something about a couple of your Alphas saving your parents, so maybe they'll be willing to help."

I shake my head. "Clearly, you don't know my parents. They'll be pissed at me for getting myself kidnapped to begin with."

She slows down now and turns to look at me. "Just leave it to me. I'll make them listen."

My mouth drops open to protest, but we have reached the office now. Diana tries the doorknob and it won't budge. It's locked.

'So much for that," I say. She rolls her eyes. There's a doormat in front of the door, which looks really weird since we are in the hall-way. The doormat says, "Wipe the shit off your shoes–there's enough shit going on in here!"

"What are you doing?" I ask her, but she doesn't answer. Instead, she just reaches under the mat and pulls out a key, which she then uses to unlock the door. "I'll be damned," I mumble. "There is someone in the world who is just as dumb as King Gene."

She laughs and puts the key back, and then we walk inside.

Sitting down at the desk, she picks up the phone and then looks at me. "What's your phone number?"

I rattle it off for her, and she dials, but I don't think this is going to work.

"Hello?" Diana says into the phone. "Yes, may I speak to the Luna or Alpha please?" She waits a moment and then says, "I'm calling with very important information from King Gene's castle regarding their next payment for their daughter's Breeder services. Yes, I'll hold."

And then, I realize what she's going to say, and it makes me really sad.

But I know it will work.

"Hello?" she says a few seconds later. I can imagine my parents running to the phone, practically tripping over one another to get there in time to get the call. "Yes, this is Clarisse from King Gene's office. I'm calling regarding the payment for Rose's Breeder services. Who am I speaking to?" There's a pause before Diana says, "Well, Luna Karen, I regret to inform you that your daughter has been kidnapped, and since she is no longer at the castle, King Gene has determined she will not be getting paid for her services anymore, and since she hasn't fulfilled her duties, you will be forced to repay all of the money he has sent you."

Diana immediately pulls the phone back away from her ear as my mother begins to scream like a lunatic. I can hear her shouting, not about me being kidnapped and in danger, but about having to repay the money.

"Listen," Diana finally shouts, "if you want to get your next payment, you'll have to figure out a way to get her out of Alpha Kane's castle and back to King Gene's. Maybe the four Alphas can help you, but I can't. Now, if I were you, I'd send someone to find one of the Alphas and let them know that Rose is being held in the castle of Alpha Kane, that he's threatening her life, and they need to hurry, got it? Otherwise, if she gets killed, you'll be on the hook for all of that money."

My mom screams a few more times before Diana says, "You heard me. You are running out of time. Goodbye." She hangs up the phone and gives me a satisfied smile.

I shake my head. "You don't know my parents. They will go hide somewhere so they don't have to repay the money or free me."

"No, they'll do it," she says confidently. I could hear it in her tone. "Don't worry. Now, let's get you back to bed." She gets up from the chair and comes around the table, and we're about to exit the room when the door opens and a familiar man is standing there.

"Well, shit," I mutter.

Diana says, "Well, shit indeed."

CHAPTER 4: CAUGHT

Eli

A sharp pain is pounding in the top of my skull. In front of me I see nothing but tree bark, so I try to turn my head, but the pain radiates even stronger. I'm guessing I hit the tree head-on, so I'm pretty amazed that I'm even awake. I move what I last remember to be my broken paw, but it's a hand now, so I must have gone unconscious and shifted back at some point.

How long have I been knocked out?

Kelly!

I have to move now since I need to see if she's okay; I need to help her. I use my good hand—which right now isn't much better than the other one—to push off the tree and try to get up and turn around at the same time. But something is stopping me.

"Piece of shit's awake," says a raspy voice right above me, and now I can feel that whoever it is, is holding me down with a huge, muddy boot.

Some dust catches in my throat, and I cough, and I'm still trying to get up or at least turn around and see who's holding me down. The male voice is definitely not familiar.

I sense someone else moving closer and another man says, "That looks like one we should worry about. Nathan! Bring the kit."

A kit—that must be a medical kit. But if they're here to help me, why is this guy holding me down with his foot?

'Kelly!' I call out in the mind-link, but she doesn't answer. I try to reach a few of the others who were with me, and all of them are quiet; I feel a knot growing in the pit of my stomach as I imagine what's happened to them. Finally, the guy lets go, and I turn around and sit up, instantly seeing why my sister and pack mates haven't responded.

They're all tied up and knocked out.

The second man laughs. "Yeah, we've got your friends, and we've got you, too," he says. "That'll teach all you fucking pack-loving rich boys to come on our territory!"

I gaze over at Kelly, who is bleeding from her head and her hands are tied behind her back. She's unconscious, and I breathe a sigh of relief when I spot the gentle rise and fall of her chest. She's alive. Apparently, she hadn't shifted, so she's fully clothed, unlike me at the moment.

The man follows my gaze, and he smiles wide to show a mouth full of rotted teeth. "Oh, you like the female, do you? She your girl?"

I glared at him and finally find my voice. "She needs medical attention!" I shout.

"Oh, she'll be fine," he says. "Head wounds are a tricky one. They look a lot worse than they are. But you have bigger problems, big man."

"Who are you?" I ask.

He laughs. "You see, that's the issue," he says. "You should know exactly who the fuck I am because I run this territory, and you're passing through it, unauthorized."

"Means ya didn't ask permission," says the first man who had put his foot on me.

"I know what it means," I say.

"Oh, Mister Smarty Pants thinks he's better than us!" hollers the first man. "Just 'cause we didn't have no ritzy school to go to don't mean you're better than us!"

"I didn't say I was," I say. I can't believe I'm wasting my time with these—rogues, they must be—when I need to get to Rose. The pain in my head is stabbing, and I feel a little sick to my stomach, but I gather my strength for the words I need to say next. "I need to know how my people are," I say with authority, using my Alpha voice. "Why are they all unconscious?"

The second man laughs. "Oh, looks like we've got an Alpha here, boys!" he says loudly, then he looks back at me. "Nathan, where the fuck are you?!"

"Here, Pete, sir!" says a young-looking boy holding an old tackle box who is running toward us.

"We have no need for Alphas here, rich boy," says the second man —Pete—as he steps back to let the boy approach.

"It kind of seems like you're the Alpha," I say. "If you're so independent, why are you together in what looks like a pack?"

I try to shift but my head is so woozy that I can't focus, and the boy, Nathan, has opened his box by now and is taking out what looks like a giant syringe.

"Hurry up," Pete tells him.

They're all starting to look fuzzy, and I take one last look over at Kelly before the world goes black.

I WAKE UP AGAIN, and this time I'm in a room of some sort, and now my head hurts even worse. I hope they didn't actually stab me with that dirty needle since I passed out on my own, although I'm afraid that's what they did to Kelly.

I look down to see that I'm wearing some tattered, dirty sweatpants, so at least I've got some clothes on, but all I can think about is Kelly, and Rose, and the rest of my people. I have to get up; I can't just lay here when they all need me.

'Kelly!' I shout again in the mind-link.

'Here,' she answers, weakly.

'Oh, thank the Goddess!' I say. 'Are you okay?'

17

'I'm all right,' she says. 'I'm somewhere in a room by myself. How about you?'

'Same,' I tell her. 'Is everyone else okay?'

'Trevor is, and a couple of the others,' she says. 'But I can't reach Ben or Liam. Their crash looked pretty bad, and I think they're....'

She trails off, but I know what she means. Though Rose and the pups are always at the forefront of my mind, my people here need me first to get them out of here... wherever 'here' is. 'What do you know about these rogues?' I ask her.

'Nothing,' she says. 'I didn't even know they were here. They have women and kids here, though. I woke up right before they took us inside, and this looks like some old, abandoned hotel or something. I never knew there was anything out here.'

'I guess we're all in separate hotel rooms then,' I say. Looking around, I can see now that the broken, dirty furniture in the room was once nice, like one would find in a luxury resort. I hadn't heard of anything like that around here, either, but then again, we're pretty far out of Gene's territory, and I'm not familiar with anything in this direction.

'Can you get up and walk around?' I ask.

'Yes, but there's a guard outside.'

'I probably have more than one, then,' I say. 'Can you shift?'

'I haven't tried. One sec,' she says. A few seconds later she says, 'Yes.'

'All right, I'll try the others.' I contact Trevor and the other warriors who'd accompanied Kelly–except for Ben and Liam, whose families I will have to contact later–and they're all in good enough shape to shift, so we discuss a plan to get the hell out of here. We're far more experienced in organized combat than a bunch of rogues, but I don't take anyone for granted who's had to fight just to stay alive for who knows how long.

Not to mention that my head is still spinning, and my hand is mangled. I'm not exactly in top shape for fighting.

The doorknob turns, and I get ready to shift, but when I see who's coming inside, I hold off. She's young, maybe about sixteen or seventeen, and she's holding a basket of what looks like medical supplies.

And she looks terrified.

She approaches me, slowly. "I—I'm here to patch up your hand," she says softly.

I nod, but don't say anything for now. Why would they send a young girl in alone with an Alpha? They've never seen me before, and I could be someone like Kane for all they know. Whoever this Pete guy is, he's risking his people for no reason.

We say nothing more as she applies an herbal salve and wraps my hand in gauze that doesn't exactly look sterile. I wonder to myself why they're wasting their supplies on me when they obviously have so little. I decide that I could probably get some information from her.

"What's your name?" I ask.

"H—Heather," she says.

"Hi Heather," I say. "I'm Eli." There's a pause while she continues wrapping my hand. "I never knew about this place," I say. "How long have you been out here?"

"I don't know," she says. "Forever, for me."

"You were born here?" I ask.

"Y—yes," she says. "I mean, that I know of. Never been nowhere else." She finishes up and closes her box, giving me a shy smile while not making eye contact before she walks out the door.

'What happened?' asks Kelly in the mind-link.

'They sent in a young girl to wrap up my hand," I say.

'A girl? Alone with a strange Alpha? Are they insane?' she asks.

'I'm starting to think that,' I say. 'We need to get the hell out of here.'

Just then the door opens again, but this time it's Pete and two tall, gangly looking men.

CHAPTER 5: IS A HAMSTER'S FOOT LUCKY?

Rose

"What the fuck are you two doing in my office?" Alpha Kane bellows as he comes charging in through the door.

"L-looking for you!" Diana says quickly. "We had an important piece of information to tell you, and Miss Rose needed to find you immediately. But obviously, you're not in here, so we decided to go back to her room and wait for you."

He seems to be pondering whether or not that could be true. "Well, what is it that you need to tell me?" He has calmed down slightly, but not much. He stands there, stroking his chin.

"Uhm, the important thing… that we need to tell you… is… uh… is….?" Diana is looking at me with a giant question mark hanging over her head, and I am at a loss for words as well, but then something comes to me.

"It's that… I think… King Gene believes you are working with Barbara against him!" There! That should be enough to get him off track about what we were actually doing in his office.

"What?" he asks, confusion washing over his face. "What do you mean? How could he possibly know that?"

"Well," I say, trying to think of a reason that would make sense.

"She... talks in her sleep, you know? And when she was trying to seduce one of my Alphas, she fell asleep. And he heard her say that she was going to kill King Gene and make you the king." I hope that half of what I am saying sounds believable. I have no idea whether Barbara talks in her sleep or not.

He stares at me, his face unwavering, for several long moments before he finally says, "That bitch!" I look at Diana, and she has a relieved expression on her face, but I don't think we're done yet. "How could she do that?"

"I don't know," I say, even though the entire story is made up. "I guess she's not as loyal to you as you had hoped she would be."

"I guess not," he says. An angry look fills his eyes, and he stares off into the distance, as if he's plotting Barbara's demise.

Outside, we hear the sounds of wolves howling and growling at one another. It sounds like the battle is getting very close to the castle. I wish I could just run out there and be taken away by my Alphas' troops, but that would be dangerous. I'm certain that Alpha Kane's men would never let me just waddle out there to the other side of the battlefront.

"Sir," Diana begins, her head tipped down as she looks reverent, "I'd hate to interrupt your thoughts, but it sounds like the battle is getting very intense out there."

"Battle?" he asks, looking up and then swiveling his head around a few times, like he's totally forgotten there was a battle going on at all. "Oh, shit! The battle! Yes, I was just coming in here to get my lucky hamster's foot."

Again, Diana and I can't help but exchange questioning looks. "Do you mean... rabbit's foot?" Diana asks him.

"No, no!" He pushes through us and walks over to his desk, where he sits down and opens up his top desk drawer. He rifles around for a minute and then pulls out a small item with a silver chain. It's hard to tell what it is from over here, and I don't want to walk over to look at it. The idea of someone carrying around the tiny foot of a hamster makes me a little sick to my stomach.

Just as he is about to get up, he glances down and sees his phone, and then his body language shifts, and he stares at it intensely.

"Is, uh, everything okay, sir?" Diana asks, and I can feel sweat beginning to pool in the small of my back. What is he looking at?

"My phone," he says. "Something is off about my phone."

"Something is off?" Diana repeats. "What do you mean?"

The sweat that has pooled in the small of my back overflows and begins to trickle down my ass, sliding down my ass crack…. My ass is sweating.

"I mean, someone has touched my phone." He lifts his eyes and looks at Diana, his stare penetrating and menacing.

I gulp down a breath and say, "Oh, you know what? When we, uh, walked over there to see if maybe you were… in the… closet, I probably bumped into it. With my giant baby belly."

His forehead furrows as he is now staring at me. "Why would you check to see if I was in the closet?" he asks me.

The closet door is behind his desk, but there's really no reason why I would have needed to walk around it to see if he was in there, not on the side of the phone anyway. It was the only excuse I could think of.

"Uh… because I thought… maybe you were in there, planning what to do with the attacking wolves. Don't you keep your secret plans in your closet like King Gene does?" I am now pulling all of this out of my ass–my sweaty ass….

"Oh," he says. "King Gene keeps secret plans in a closet in his office?"

I nod. "That is my understanding."

"Interesting. I will have to let Barbara know that so she can get in there and find those secret plans. Now, you've really helped me, stupid, fat, pregnant lady." He gives me a wicked grin and then reaches over and straightens his phone.

I want to punch him in the nose for calling me all of those names, but I have to remember that he is an idiot, and idiots are bound to say stupid things.

Diana grabs my hand. "We have to get back to Rose's room now. The babies need to take a nap."

"All right," he says. "Thank you for helping me with all of this valuable information, Rose. I may not kill all of your babies in front of you now. I may take them into another room to kill them."

"You're a fucking saint," I tell him as Diana pulls me out of the room.

As we walk along, she says, "Be cool. You can't let him make you mad. That's what he's trying to do. Besides, if you listen to what's going on outside, I think your Alphas are making good headway. It sounds like there's a ton of screaming going on out there, and I doubt that your Alphas' troops are going to be screaming like little pups."

She has a good point. I don't want to go back to my assigned room and wait for the Alphas to rescue me. No, I want to go running out to meet them, but I know that is a mistake. I have to stay here and be patient.

I have to trust that my men will come for me, sooner or later.

And I have to trust that they will get here in time to save me and their children.

CHAPTER 6: SHE'S NOT HERE

TRISTAN

Reece, Mark, and I have shifted and are running full speed toward Stephen's castle. There is no way any of us were going to sit patiently on a military vehicle and wait to arrive by truck. No, we're going in fast, and we're going in now.

We're surrounded by our best warriors. Though some of those have certainly gone to fight Kane in the first company, we always retain a few great fighters for our second contingent. The tactic helps us resupply our ranks with strong, fresh fighters when our first troops need a rest. In this case, they're going to be on the front lines taking care of Stephen while the others start in on Kane.

We need to find out whether Rose is here at Stephen's castle or not.

I don't believe Barbara for one second, but it makes sense to check here first since it's only a bit off our direct path to Kane. Wherever she is, none of us want Rose and the pups waiting needlessly.

I'm thankful for the run. I need to work off some of this rage I've been building up since I first found out that Rose had been kidnapped. No doubt, I'll get a great workout when the fighting starts, but right now, this is a different kind of release. I need to clear my head so that

I won't make any mistakes, and feeling the soft grass on my paws as I run forward at top speed is somehow therapeutic.

With my concentration so intense, we arrive before it feels like much time has passed at all. All looks quiet, and all of us shift back to human form while our assistants, who have run along with us holding our supply packs, provide us with sweatpants. Now, we switch to walking as we approach the castle walls while checking out the perimeter. We hadn't brought the plans to Stephen's castle back in Gene's library because we'd been certain about our target—Kane—so we are going in a bit less prepared for this military operation.

If I had any qualms at all about our lack of preparation, they're all washing away now as Stephen's 'warriors' approach. By their body language and obvious lack of confidence, it's clear that they've had little, if any, training in anything related to combat. We have nothing to worry about.

"Halt!" says the first guard in a shaky, squeaky voice. "State your name and purpose!"

He stops about twenty yards away, close enough to see into his eyes, which betray his trembling fear.

"We are Alphas Tristan, Reece, and Mark, and we demand to see Alpha Stephen immediately!" I say in my most authoritative Alpha voice.

The man's eyes widen, and he starts to open his mouth but then stops, turns, and heads back into the castle. I look over at Reece and Mark, and Mark shrugs. We wait for a moment, and I send one of my warriors around to the side to assess the integrity of the outer wall while the other Alphas and I communicate with our troops, who have almost arrived.

Finally, the gate opens again, and the first man comes out, followed by several others—in fact, they're piling out of there like bees coming out of a hive. The other Alphas and I hold our ground while Stephen's people form a line—at least they're halfway disciplined—and stand at attention. Soon the inner part of the crowd breaks away to form a path, and Alpha Stephen finally appears looking old, tired, and grumpy.

"What's going on?!" he shouts. When he sees me and the other Alphas, I can sense fear, but not the level of fear I'm expecting.

'He should be terrified if he's got Rose,' says Reece in the mind-link.

'Agreed,' says Mark. 'He's scared, but something's not right.'

"I hope to the fucking Goddess that you've come to take back that bitch," Stephen says. "Unfortunately, you're a little too late."

My wolf snarls inside me. Too late?! "Where is she?!" I scream.

"She escaped," he says. "And frankly, good fucking riddance."

"Escaped?" asks Mark. "When?"

We all look at each other again, confused. We should have heard Rose in the mind-link if she'd escaped. And if she has gotten away, she's out there in the wild forest all alone. Why hasn't she called for help? I can tell the same question is going through the other Alphas' minds.

"Oh, I don't know," says Stephen casually. "It's been so fucking quiet and peaceful since then; I didn't keep track of the time."

"What?" asks Reece.

"Quiet," he says. "It's like when there's no rude, crude bitch constantly in your ear asking for clothes or food or jewelry or money or fucking anything else in the world. I don't think I could have stood it for a moment longer anyway. So, since she's not here, you might as well leave."

"What about the babies?" asks Mark. "Are they okay? Did she go into labor?"

"What?!" asked Stephen. "She's pregnant?"

"Um…"

"She's huge with child," I say. "You can't possibly miss that. She's having four of them."

"Four of them!" says Stephen. "Wow!" A smile grows on his face, and I'm about to punch him. "I didn't know I was so… productive."

At that, I do step forward and punch him, and he spins around and falls on the ground. His troops look terrified at first, then they seem to realize that they have to do something, so they surround us, but they still hold back and don't actually do anything. My warriors stand at attention but don't approach; they know when I want to handle something myself.

"What the fuck was that for?" Stephen asks.

"That's just a portion of what you're going to get for touching her, you piece of shit," I say. "She's an innocent woman, and pregnant with innocent pups who have nothing to do with your power lust. I'm going to tear you to shreds for laying a finger on her."

"Well, fuck," he says. "She IS my wife, technically."

"What?!" asks Reece.

If there's a time when I'd actually have steam coming out of my ears, it's now. He forced Rose to marry him?!

"She's technically my wife, so I can certainly touch her if I want to," he says again. "And I didn't know you gave a rat's ass about Emily."

We all just stand there, staring at him. A wave of relief washes over me as Stephen keeps talking.

"How would you know she's pregnant anyway? I haven't seen any of you hanging around here."

'Thank the Goddess,' says Mark in the mind-link. 'He's talking about Emily. I was ready to kill him.'

'Me, too,' I say. 'Although this doesn't mean that Rose isn't here.'

'I'm not getting that vibe,' Reece says. 'But we should search the place anyway.'

I nod, and Stephen looks at me, confused.

"We're going to need to search your castle," I say.

"What?!" he hollers. "Why?"

"If Rose is in there, I highly recommend that you bring her out to us at once," says Reece. "We won't have much mercy if we find her tied up somewhere inside."

Tied up... just the phrase gives me a sharp pain in my gut. I need to find my little flower, and now.

"Rose?" Stephen asks. "You mean your fucking Breeder? You will not be searching my private castle, regardless."

"We will," I say firmly, moving in until my face is only inches from his own. A bead of sweat forms on his temple and flows down the side of his cheek, and I can feel his heart pounding hard.

"You and what army?" he says, his voice wavering a little, but he's still holding his ground.

Just then, the first group of our second contingent rolls over the hill formed by the dirt road leading to the castle. One after another, more vehicles arrive until the entire field surrounding his castle is filled with soldiers.

"That would be that army," I say plainly.

Stephen takes a couple of deep breaths and then looks down at the ground. "Oh, go ahead," he says. "What do I care? Just don't break anything. That bitch Emily broke plenty of priceless art pieces already."

Reece, Mark, and I start instructing our warriors to search the castle, and Stephen calls off his people. His raggedy group of soldiers all look relieved beyond measure as they file back behind the castle walls. I'm just about to enter myself when I hear an unfamiliar voice calling in the mind-link.

"Alpha Tristan? Alpha Mark? Alpha Reece?" says the voice.

The other Alphas and I all look at each other, then we notice someone running, coming from a strange car that's parked in the middle of our military vehicles. He runs forward and finally reaches us, completely out of breath.

"I'm supposed… to deliver… this… message…," he says between exhausted breaths, "in person."

"We're the Alphas," I say. "What is it?"

"It's Miss… Miss Rose's parents," he says.

"What?!" I say. I can't imagine Rose's parents would ever have the nerve to contact us again.

"She…."

"She what?" asks Reece.

The man is clearly out of breath, and it takes him a bit to compose himself and answer, "Miss Rose sent a message."

CHAPTER 7: UP TO MY EYEBALLS

Barbara

They're going to figure out that I lied to them, and then… well, I'm going to be in deep, deep doo-doo.

Not to mention the fact that Kane is supposed to be storming this castle already, and he's not.

I need to convince Gene to do something that will throw the Alphas off, but when I knock on his open office door, he is asleep on his desk, his head folded on his arms, drool dripping out of the corner of his mouth.

He is a helpless man-child, and I absolutely hate him. I hate Kane, too, but I also love him, and that may seem complicated, but it's the truth.

Gene, on the other hand, I am ready to shake until his head wobbles loose and then springs free of his neck and rolls around the floor. At least he bought my story about someone else being responsible for killing that guard. He is such a fucking moron.

So I can't help but stand in the doorway and scream his name at the top of my lungs to jar him awake. "Gene!" I shout.

He leaps up, banging his knee on the bottom of his desk, shouting, "Mommy?" followed quickly by, "Ouch!"

I shake my head as he stands there and rubs his leg. He narrows his gaze at me. "You're not my mommy–mother. What are you doing in my office, Barbara? You know I can't be tempted by your seductering ways."

I roll my eyes at him. "I'm not trying to seduce you, Your Majesty." It kills me a bit on the inside to have to call him that. "I just came to ask you what your plan is when those Alphas find Rose and come back here to fight you."

His eyebrows knit together as he stares at me, clearly dumbfounded. "Rose?" he repeats. He reaches up and strokes his chin. "Do I know a Rose?"

I want to punch him in his dumb head.

"Yeah, you do. She's the Breeder," I remind him.

"Oh, right. That Rose," he says. "I'm confused. I thought that Kane was going to wait until those babies crawled out of her and then kill them all. What's taking him so long? Can't he force the babies to crawl out? Can't he just bend down and shout up her va-jay-jay and order them to come out? Or is he just not as powerful as I am?"

I stare at him, feeling rather dumb myself now. Is it possible that anyone can be as stupid as he is? "How many times did your mother drop you on your head when you were a baby?" I ask him.

He blinks at me a few times, shrugs, and says, "Well, I don't know, Barbara. I was a baby. Babies are dumb. I wouldn't remember that."

My gut feeling tells me that it's a lot. He probably fell off of the bed onto his head on the daily for a few years to be this stupid.

"King Gene," I say, closing the distance between us, "this is serious. Those Alphas are going to be pissed when they get back here, especially if something does happen to those babies or that woman. Listen, you started all of this, right? It was your idea to bring them here and to bring her here. Now, you've got to get your shit together to fight against them."

He looks like he's about to say something smart to me, but then his forehead crinkles, and he's rubbing his chin again. "You know, I've never thought about that. Is that... an option? I wasn't aware that... shit could fight."

"What?" I ask him, thinking I can't actually be hearing this.

"I mean… it is part of me. I always just flush it away, but maybe I should just fish it out and give it a chance to crawl around, like those babies. Maybe it could fight, too?"

I feel like I might throw up, envisioning him fishing his shit out of the toilet and trying to train it to fight on his behalf. "I know you are the king, and I'm meant to respect you," I begin, "but you are one sick, idiotic motherfucker," I tell him.

He stares at me wide eyed. "How dare you!"

"Listen, I'm trying to help you. Did you know that there's a secret passage where the door leads out into the middle of the forest? Just about anyone could come into the castle that way, and Kane knows where it is."

He swats at me with his hand. "Yes, I know about that door. But don't worry. It's locked."

"It's not locked!" I tell him. "I know because I–" I stop myself as I realize I can't tell him the truth, and I don't want to be as stupid as he is. "I know because Kane told me. Even if it was locked, it wouldn't be too difficult for a competent Alpha to lead his army through that door and right into your castle."

I have to specify a competent Alpha because I don't know why Kane hasn't done this already. He certainly didn't need the key, and he certainly didn't need me to be the guinea pig.

"Do you really think those big, bad Alphas are going to be coming for me?" King Gene asks, and he looks a bit terrified.

"Yes, I do!" I tell him, my arms flailing in frustration. "I do think they will come for you, and I do think that you need to figure out what you're going to do about it. If you have any other allies out there, you'd better call them and get them over here stat."

"That's easy enough," he says with a shrug. "I've got Alpha Kane."

"No, you don't!" I shout at him. "Alpha Kane is not your ally! He is planning on storming this castle through that door I just told you about as soon as he figures out what to do with Rose and the attacking Alphas. I'm telling you, Gene, you've got to figure this out! Do you have any other Alphas that are still loyal to you, or are all of them only interested in the throne?"

Sweat is beading on his forehead as he stares over his desk at me, shaking his head. "I... I don't know." His bottom lip protrudes, and he looks like he's about to cry.

"Now is the time to find out!" I tell him. "Call them. Pick up the fucking phone and call the people you think might help you."

That's it. That's all I can do. I know how to get out of this castle. I need to seriously consider what my next move is. Do I really want to be here when the shit hits the fan? No, I really don't, especially if the shit just happens to be his own poop balls he's fished out of the toilet.

Nope. I'm out.

I turn and walk back to my room, but I can't just run away at this point. I have my own army, but it's small, and so far, they've been practically useless. I have my own pack, but they can easily be over-run. That means... I'm in a precarious position, and I've got to be careful, or I'm going to end up in just as deep a pile of shit as Gene.

And I don't like to play with my poo....

CHAPTER 8: KANE HAS ANOTHER VICTIM

KELLY

'Someone's here,' Eli says in the mind-link, and then things go quiet, which can't be good. But all I can do is wait until he can talk to me again.

I look around at my surroundings again, and I realize what a nice hotel this once was. The furniture is made from solid oak, and it looks like someone spent a lot of money on all the details, everything from the bedding to the beautiful art that now dangles crooked on the walls.

They probably spent too much money, and that's why it was abandoned. But what's important right now isn't the building's past but how we can manage to escape from it.

I peek out into the hallway, and finding no one, I sneak over to the room where I'd left Trevor. Whoever these people are, they're not guarding us individually, but apparently, the entire floor has guards at either side. I'd been trying the windows in every room, and so far, none of them open. I guess they didn't want guests falling out of the windows in this old resort.

I've been up and down this entire floor, and they're not holding Eli here, so they must have some special guards on him. It's obvious he's the Alpha, so that does make sense. But if I can't get out any windows here, and they're guarding all the exits, I'm not sure how we'll get to him anyway.

"He went silent," says Trevor when I walk in.

"I know," I say. "And I don't like it at all."

"I'm sure he just needs to focus," he says.

"Probably, but I'm still worried," I say. "His hand is in pretty bad shape."

Trevor nods. "Any luck with the windows?" he asks.

"Nope," I say. "There aren't any that open; they're all just pretty picture windows for looking at the forest, which admittedly is a great view."

"I've never heard of this place before," he says. "But it was probably pretty nice in its day."

The door opens, and we both spin around to look, ready to shift, but it's just the other warriors who had come with us to find Eli—Brent and Sean.

"Shit, you scared me," I say. "Knock maybe?"

They both nod and plop down in the chairs. "No luck," says Brent. "There's a fire escape, but you have to get through to the stairwell, and they have two guys guarding it."

"Well, there are four of us," I say. "So what's the problem?"

"None, except that we're all generally injured, and whatever they shot us up with is making me woozy," he says.

"I have to admit, I'm feeling that, too," says Trevor. "But we need to get to Alpha Eli. We didn't come all the way out here to rescue him just to lose him again."

"Agreed," I say. "But we need a solution. So, two guys are guarding the stairs. I saw just one on the other side, but that's just on our floor. I'm not sure how many guards would be in the rest of the stairway."

"Well, I'd rather fight two I'm sure of than one after another," says Sean.

I have to agree with him. "So what do these guys look like?" I ask.

"Like they're starving," Brent says. "I'm pretty sure all these people have been here for a long time. You'd think there'd be a lot of game around here, so I don't know what's up with that."

"It's the stupid rules." I heard her voice before she even started entering the room since the guys had left the door ajar.

We all prepare to shift, but when we see her, we realize she's only a kid, maybe sixteen or so. I relax a little but stay alert and walk over to her, peering through the door to be sure she doesn't have backup, which she doesn't, so I close it behind her. We don't need any more surprises.

"What kind of rules?" asks Trevor.

"Stupid ones," she answers. "Rules that say only the hunters can hunt, for one. We're all perfectly capable of shiftin' and huntin' a meal, but Alpha Pete's got it in his head that we all need special duties."

"I didn't peg any of these guys for an Alpha," I say.

"That's 'cause he's not," she says.

"Rogues wouldn't have an Alpha anyway," says Trevor.

The girl knitted up her brow and glared at him. "We ain't rogues!" she hollered.

"All right," I say calmly, not wanting to upset her more. She is clearly far too young to be sent to check on a bunch of prisoners by herself, so someone here isn't treating her very well. I thought about what Eli told me about the girl who they'd sent in with him. She must be the same girl. "You're a pack, then. What's the pack name?"

"Stone Creek pack," she says, pronouncing the E in Creek like it is an I. "This is our territory, and Alpha Pete got pissed off that you kept driving through like we was nothing."

"Alpha Pete…" I say. "You say he's not an Alpha, yet you call him one?"

The girl nods and looks like tears are about to form in her eyes as she says, "His cousin was Alpha Andrew. He got shot."

My heart skips a couple of beats, wondering if our captors have weapons.

"They came here and took him, hauled him up to a tree, and shot him!" she says, and then the tears flow. "He was my Pa." She plops down in a chair and puts her face in her hands while she sobs.

"You're the Alpha's daughter?" I say softly. She nods, then I continue, "Who did that to him?"

The girl looks up at me, and a change has come over her; her eyes are glazed over from tears, but I can clearly see the anger in them. "Kane," she says softly.

"Alpha Kane killed your father?" I ask. "Why?"

"I don't know," she says. "I was just a pup. But I remember clear as day when his blood splattered all over everywhere."

I pull a chair up next to her and put my arm around her. "I'm so sorry that happened to you, dear," I say. "What's your name?"

"Heather," she says.

"Heather, that's a pretty name," I say. "I'm Kelly, and this is Trevor, Brent, and Sean. We're not here to hurt anyone in your pack. We came to rescue my brother from someone who was holding him several miles from here."

"Your brother?" she asks, her sobs slowing. It was clear that no one had spoken to her in a gentle way for years.

"He's the one you patched up," I say. "He really appreciated your help, too. You did a great job."

"You mean, the mean Alpha is your brother?" she asks.

I shake my head. "He's not mean," I say. "And I should know. I grew up with him." I smile at her, and she smiles back weakly.

"Then he can't be mean, then," she says.

Trevor and the others have backed away, sensing that the girl needs some time talking to a woman. So they sit across the room, trying their best to look non-threatening. That's a challenge for Brent, who's over six-foot-six and pretty muscular, being one of our best warriors. I can also sense that the girl and her pack—if that's what this truly is—need some serious help. We'll have to help her, but we're running out of time to get to Rose.

"Heather," I say. "We really need your help here. You see, we have a common enemy, and we don't have a lot of time."

"Common enemy?" she asks.

I nod. "Alpha Kane."

Her eyes widen and she wipes away the last remnant of a tear on her cheek. "You're gonna fight Alpha Kane?"

"Yes," I say. "And we need to do it fast. He's holding someone hostage that we love very much, and we need to rescue her."

"Her?"

I nod again. "Yes, she's a woman, and she's going to have pups any minute now, so we need to get to her quickly. Can you get us out of here? I know you need help, and I promise that we'll come and help you just as soon as we're done dealing with Kane."

"I've heard that before," she says, sinking back into her chair, looking dejected.

"Someone promised to help before?" I ask.

She nods. "Alpha Kane," she says. "But then he and my pa argued about something, and he shot him!"

"I'm so sorry about that, Heather," I say. "But we're nothing like that awful Alpha Kane."

"I know," she says. "It's just, you might get hurt and not come back if you're fightin' him."

"We'll come back," I say.

And I mean it. Whatever is happening with this girl and her pack, they desperately need someone powerful to step in and handle things. Sure, this is a luxury hotel, but it's been a long time since it was restocked with supplies, and this Pete person seems like he's gone off the deep end, yet they're stuck with him as a leader.

She looks up at me for a while as if she's trying to figure it out, then she takes a deep breath. "I know where your Alpha is," she says. "I'll take you to him."

CHAPTER 9: TO TRUST OR NOT TO TRUST

Mark

"Miss Rose sent a message."

The words of the messenger running from the car toward us hit me right in the heart. "Rose sent a message?" we all repeat in one way or another. Our mission to storm Alpha Stephen's castle looking for her has momentarily been put on hold. Unless, of course, this messenger says she's being held within the castle, which I doubt at this point.

He is out of breath, and the fact that he is panting is annoying all of us as we wish he'd just spit it out, whatever it is.

"Use the mind-link if you have to!" Tristan shouts at him.

But by now, he seems to be able to breathe again. "She's being held captive in Alpha Kane's castle," he finally says, still doubled-over.

"Alpha Kane has her?" Reece presses. "You're certain?"

"That's what she said." He's able to straighten up a bit. "That's the message her parents received."

We all look at one another. Can her parents be trusted? After all, they were never kind to Rose. We wouldn't put it past them to join with Kane to make things difficult for us.

"I don't understand why they suddenly care," Tristan says, looking at Reece and I and then back to the messenger.

"Yeah, it's just not adding up," I agree. "They have never shown an interest in Rose before."

"Maybe this is just a ruse, arranged by Alpha Stephen, to get us to leave his castle without looking inside of it." Reece scratches his chin in deep thought. "Not that I necessarily think that Stephen is smart enough to come up with that."

"This is true," Tristan says. "It's not like we can even tell for certain that this guy is from Rose's parents' pack." He hooks a thumb at the messenger.

"Excuse me, sirs," the man says. "I hate to interrupt, but I am from Rose's parents' pack." He shows us the shoulders of his uniform, which contain the emblem of the Elm pack. "But more importantly, I can assure you that it's real. I overheard the Luna and Alpha discussing whether or not to try to locate the three of you—well, the four of you." He looks around, as if he is confused that one of us is missing, and another pang hits me. We do miss Eli and are worried about him, though Rose is our primary concern.

"Go on," Tristan prods. "You overheard them saying what, exactly?"

He nods, as if bringing his thoughts back around. "I overheard them saying that they need the money, and they were told by whomever delivered the message on Miss Rose's behalf, if they didn't get her back to King Gene's castle, they wouldn't be eligible for the payment for her Breeder services that is due soon. So, you see, it's not concern for their daughter that had them sending me over to find you. It's greed. Now, surely, that must make sense to all of you."

Again, we exchange glances, and the messenger, who seems sincere, and a little bitter, looks ready to dart back to the waiting car and get out of here. After all, he and his driver have just driven through what is about to be a war zone.

"I think we should move to Alpha Kane's castle," Tristan says. "We can leave some of our warriors here to surround Alpha Stephen's castle and make sure that he isn't a threat, but the three of us should rush over to Alpha Kane's and see if Rose is truly there."

"If she is, I will personally rip his head off," Reece says, his eyes narrowing.

"I'm gonna tear his dick off and shove it down his throat," Tristan adds, and I am left wondering if he will do that before or after Reece rips his head off.

They both look at me, like they are waiting for me to chime in. I can respond only, "I want him dead, too. I don't care how it happens."

Turning to the messenger, I say, "Thank you. You can go." Normally, I would offer someone like this a tip, but I don't have any money in the pockets of the sweatpants I've been handed.

Tristan signals to one of his men who is standing nearby, and the assistant steps forward with some bills that he hands to the messenger. That makes his face light up. "Thank you kindly, sirs," he says before heading back to the car.

"He may not actually go back to his pack with that kind of a tip," Reece notes.

Tristan shrugs. "If what he says is true, and Rose is at Alpha Kane's–alive–and we can save her and the pups, then that guy deserves a hell of a lot more than that."

I definitely agree with him. We hold our soldiers at bay as the car turns around and heads back the direction it came from.

"All right," Tristan says as the car roars away. "We need to get to Rose as soon as we can. Let's just leave a few smaller units here to inspect the castle and keep Stephen from leaving."

"Sounds good," Reece and I tell him. I contact one of my commanders and give him the plan, then, I order the others to follow me.

Less than five minutes after the messenger from Rose's home pack drove away, the three of us have shifted, and we are running swiftly to Alpha Kane's castle. The battle is already underway there as we sent a lot of our warriors in that direction because we thought there was a good chance Kane had her. This is just further proof that Barbara is lying.

As I am running through the forest, dodging bushes and fallen tree limbs, I send a mind-link message to Adam. "Keep an eye on Barbara," I tell him. "We are pretty sure that she lied to us about Alpha Stephen having Rose on purpose. She seems to know that Rose is at Alpha Kane's castle. I'm certain she's still working with Alpha Kane."

He sounds exhausted when his voice fills my mind. "All right," he says. "I'll keep an eye on her. King Gene seems to be suffering from dementia. Most of the things coming out of his mouth now don't even make sense."

I am sad to hear that anyone is suffering from that awful disease, but considering his mother obviously has it, I'm not too surprised. "Keep an eye on him, too. He might decide to do something stupid."

Adam replies, "I'm afraid it's a little too late for that. He's always doing something stupid."

I know that to be the truth as well.

We spend a couple of hours running, and then the sounds of battle hit our ears. Up in front of us, I see the top of Alpha Kane's modest castle jutting out of the mountain top and know we are almost there.

Rose is here. I can sense her.

"I'm coming for you, baby!" I tell her, not using the mind-link because I've been unable to reach her, but I'm telling her with my heart and soul.

I will find her, I will make sure she's safe, and then, I will make Kane pay.

CHAPTER 10: NEVER LIE TO THE ALPHA

Adam

Well, shit.

Lying to your Alpha is the number one thing that a good Beta should never do.

Technically, Alpha Mark is not my Alpha, at least not right now, and I'm not technically his Beta, and I technically didn't lie. I said I'd keep an eye on her, and I will. Just as soon as I find her.

Too many damn technicalities.

Well, first things first... I have to find Barbara so I can keep an eye on her. She was endlessly bitching about her clothes, so I don't know why she wouldn't want to follow me to the seamstress. That is, after all, the only way she's going to get new clothes. I honestly don't understand women.

But... I know someone who does.

'Shelby, my love,' I call out sweetly in the mind-link. She loves when I do that.

'What?' she asks as a response.

Goddess, her voice is sexy. 'I need your help,' I say. 'I kind of... lost track of Barbara.'

'What?!' I hate when she mind-link screams.

'I know,' I say. 'I don't know what happened. She was right behind me, and now she's gone.'

'Well,' Shelby says, sounding a bit agitated, but even that sounded sexy. 'Where was she last?'

'Following me to the sewing room,' I say. 'She was complaining about her clothes to Gene, then he ordered me to take her there, then she just kind of stopped following me.'

'How did you not sense that she was gone?' Shelby asks.

Well, I don't want to answer that. I know she likes that I think about her all the time, but this isn't the time for that with Rose missing. The thoughts of Shelby's beautiful body were definitely distracting me before I noticed Barbara was missing. 'I don't know,' I say. I'm lying again, and this time to my mate. I think that's worse than lying to an Alpha.

'Well, look in the spot she was where you last saw her,' she says. 'I'll be right there.'

My heart jumps a bit inside knowing that my mate is coming to be by my side, but I admonish myself because that thing that I'm quite sure she was thinking while I spoke to her is right. Now is not the time to act like love-sick pups.

So, I retrace my steps, heading back toward Gene's living quarters. Maybe she had some unfinished business with him and figured I would just somehow handle her clothes by myself. I don't understand women at all. Was I supposed to try them on for the seamstress myself?

As I approach Gene's room, I hear Barbara's grating, scratchy voice. I sigh in relief, although I can't believe I'm happy to hear that torturing sound. At least I know where she is, and I can do what I told Mark I would—keep an eye on her.

I get just up to the doorway when I hear Barbara say, "Did you know that there's a secret passage where the door leads out into the middle of the forest? Just about anyone could come into the castle that way, and Kane knows where it is."

I freeze in my tracks and slowly back away from the door. I know the Alphas will want to know whatever Barbara knows about Kane, so

I need to hear this without her knowing I'm here. I back up, painfully slowly, being careful to take a step whenever one of them speaks to muffle the sound. When I feel pretty confident that I'm far enough away, I listen.

She's talking about the secret passageway, and some sort of door that's not really locked but sounds like it should be.

And Kane knows where it is. And he's planning on storming the castle.

After being jolted by that news, I feel warmth enter the hall and inhale my mate's scent. I want to close my eyes and enjoy the sensation, but instead I turn around and hold one finger against my mouth to indicate that she should be quiet. She nods and carefully walks up to me, her footfalls completely silent. How she does that in those shoes, I have no idea.

She puts her arm around me when she reaches me and listens to the tail end of the conversation between Gene and Barbara.

'She's coming,' Shelby tells me in the mind-link, and we move around the doorway and hide just as Barbara comes out of Gene's room in a huff, which is generally her natural state.

'What do we do?' asks Shelby in the mind-link as Barbara walks down the hallway.

'We follow her, and we tell the Alphas,' I say.

Barbara is walking quickly now, and it seems that she's headed back to her room. I guess the whole clothes issue is out the window now. Shelby and I hold back until she's around the corner, then we tiptoe to the end of the hallway and peer around into the next one, catching sight of Barbara just as she rounds the next corner.

We follow her this way for a while before she goes into her room and slams the door shut. I can hear rummaging around in there and wonder what she's up to.

'She's packing,' says Shelby in the mind-link, although I hadn't asked her what she thought was going on. I guess she reads my mind all the time.

'To warn Kane,' I say, then I think of the Alphas and call out to them.

They answer, one by one.

'What is it?' asks Alpha Tristan.

'Kane,' I say. 'Barbara was talking to Gene. Kane knows about the secret passageways, and apparently, he knows about some door in a tunnel out in the forest that may or may not be locked. He's planning on storming the castle.'

'Well,' says Alpha Tristan, 'he's not doing it now, because his full forces are right here in front of us.'

'And Barbara is trying to leave, or escape, or whatever you'd call it,' I say, adding to my report.

'Do you have any warriors there that you trust?' he asks.

I do know Gene's warriors well, and I know the difference between the ones who would truly die for the crown and those who would most likely be working for Kane right now. 'A few,' I say.

'Put them on her,' Alpha Tristan says. 'You stay there and watch Gene... and find that damn door. If we can seal it off, that would help.'

'Be careful,' Alpha Mark adds. 'We really have no idea how many troops Kane has, so he may have sent a few to infiltrate the castle. As much as I think Gene is a cruel idiot, we need him to stay alive for now.'

'Agreed,' says Alpha Reece. 'For all we know, Kane took Rose as a distraction to get us here and away from there.'

'Better put some guards on Gene,' Alpha Tristan says. 'We're about to hit the action here, so we have to go.'

'Goddess be with you,' I say, and I put my head down to say a silent prayer. Shelby does the same, even though she hadn't been in on the conversation. I guess she knows that everything going on right now is potentially deadly.

I message a few of the warriors I trust and instruct them to get to the king's quarters immediately and not leave until I'm there personally.

"The whole kidnapping could be a ruse to get the castle empty," I say to Shelby in a whisper. "I've sent men to guard Gene, and I'll send a few to keep an eye on Barbara as well, then we need to find that damn door."

I send another message to different warriors to come to guard Barbara, then we wait for the warriors to arrive. I instruct them to enter the room if they stop hearing her in there—for all we know, there's a secret exit right there in Barbara's room.

Now, it's our turn to act. The only entrances to the secret passageway that I'm certain of are in the library, Gene's room, and Rose's room. Since Rose's room is so far away from here, and we can't go explain any of this to Gene in his state of mind, I take Shelby's hand, interlock our fingers, and run toward the library.

I hope we're not running to our deaths.

CHAPTER 11: ODDS AREN'T GOOD

ROSE

It's clear to Diana and I that there's a battle raging outside of the castle, and I want desperately to get out of here, to try to get to my Alphas, so that we can all be together again.

Well, most of us. I still don't know if Eli has been found yet, but I feel deep inside of me that he hasn't been. I can sense that the other three Alphas are nearby. It's part of our bond, I believe. Perhaps it's our children calling to their fathers. But Eli seems to be missing, and it hurts my heart.

We are back in the room that I woke up in a little while ago, standing near the window. "It's good that we are in the castle instead of out there on the battlefield," Diana begins. "Actually, it's good that we are behind Alpha Kane's troops and not in front of them."

"Why do you say that?" I ask her, confused. I see a wall of wolves standing in front of the castle, but I can't see what they are preparing for yet, and the glass is so thick, it's hard to hear anything.

"Because… Alpha Kane plays dirty," she says. "Do you see all those humans standing nearer to the castle?"

"Yes," I tell her, my eyes honing in on them. "What about them?"

"Those are the snipers," she says, shaking her head.

"Snipers?" I ask. A wave of fear washes over me, settling deep inside of my gut, twisting into a knot. "Do you mean...?" Before I can even finish the question or wait for her to respond, I see exactly what she's talking about. The sun gleams off black steel.

Guns.

The humans haven't shifted into their wolf forms because they are armed with guns. "He always does that," Diana says, looking morose. "He knows he can't win if he plays by the rules, so he cheats. He has armed men standing by, ready to shoot the wolves with silver bullets as they attack his forces."

My knees grow weak just thinking about the damage that could be done by a bullet ripping through one of my Alphas. I grapple for the windowsill, trying to keep on my feet.

Diana sees me struggling and reaches over, taking hold of my arm. "Are you all right?" she asks me.

I shake my head. "No. I feel like I'm going to vomit," I admit. "What if one of my Alphas gets killed?" Even the thought of their warriors being shot up makes me ill.

"I know. It's terrible," Diana says. "But you can't get word to them because Alpha Kane is scrambling your thoughts, right? He won't allow you to use the mind-link."

"That's right." I sink down into a chair near the window, my hands rubbing my bulging belly. "There's got to be some way to get word to them, though."

Diana shrugs. "Even if there is, do you think it would make a difference? I mean, they are Alphas, on their way to save you, right? There's already a battle raging on the other side of the castle with their advanced troops, and they are doing well there. You could tell them that Alpha Kane has called out his sharpshooters, but I doubt they'd slow down their running to get here."

She might be right, but still, I have to try. "Why isn't he shooting at them?" I ask.

"He knows if he lets the shooters fire before the Alphas get here, they'll hear the gunfire or be told about the shootings from their advanced forces. So they'll slow up, and then he won't have a chance to take out the big dogs."

"My Alphas," I correct her, and she nods. "We have to do something!" I try to push up to standing again, but I can't. I'm too weak, and the babies are scrambling inside of me, seeming to be playing a game of Twister.

"I'm sorry, Rose. I wish I could help you again, but I don't think I can this time." Diana looks sympathetically at me, and I think she is actually trying to help, to be a friend to me.

I think for a moment about what to do. I try to reach the Alphas again, but it's clear that Alpha Kane is still doing that thing that prevents me from being able to use my mind-link. "Shit," I mutter.

"Alphas have a lot of power when it comes to mind-links," she says. "Especially when someone is in their pack, under their control."

"You can say that again," I agree as some sound finally does filter into me, and I hear howls in the distance. I wonder if I could open the window and shout to them. "Maybe you could sneak out and tell them!" I say, tugging on her arm.

"Uhm, no, I don't think that's a good idea," she says. "They won't know I'm there to help, and they'll run me over."

"You could tell them with the mind-link that you're on their side before they reach you!" I suggest. "They're all Alphas. They'll be able to hear you!"

"Wait!" she says. "You're right. They are all Alphas. I don't need to go out there at all to reach them! Assuming Alpha Kane hasn't caught on to the fact that I'm helping you yet, he's not scrambling my mind-link. I can reach out to them!"

I feel stupid for not having thought of that before. "Of course, you can!" I smack myself in the forehead. "Their names are Alpha Tristan, Alpha Mark, and Alpha Reece. See if you can reach them! Tell them I'm here and about the guns."

Diana nods, and I pray she's able to reach them... and that I can trust her.

I can trust her, can't I?

A few moments later, Diana is nodding. "Okay," she tells me. "I was able to get through to all three of them, and I told them about the guns and where you are."

"Thank the Moon Goddess!" I exclaim. "What are they going to do?"

"I'm not sure," she says. "It's not like they easily trusted me when I said I was on your side. So... I'm sure they'll have to decide that without me."

"Well, at least they know now." I smile optimistically at her. I'm hoping that it's enough. "Thank you."

"Sure," she says. "But... when you leave here, you're taking me with you, right?"

"Of course!" I assure her. "You should probably go pack your bags."

She snickers. "I don't have anything worth taking."

That makes me sad, but I can empathize. I've been there myself.

Outside of the window, I hear more howling... and then... a barrage of gunfire. I close my eyes tightly, afraid to look.

What if they all die?

CHAPTER 12: NOT JUST A BREEDER

Eli

"Well, I hope you're… comfortable, Alpha," says Pete.

The two men behind him chuckle a little, and I assess the situation. Clearly, they're trying to intimidate me, but they're falling a little short. The main guy, Pete, is obviously not an Alpha, but he's trying to act like one. And the other two look like they'd be formidable if they weren't practically starving, but it's clear they've missed far too many meals to be in good shape.

Who are these people?

"It's a nice place," I say, deciding to be friendly. Rogues can be unpredictable, and I don't want to be more combative than I have to, at least not until I know what's going on with Kelly and the others. It's not a lie; it is a nice place, or at least it was, back when this resort was new.

Pete doesn't seem to like my tactic, though, and he moves in closer, looking at me with knitted brows. "You tryin' to make fun of us, Alpha?" I notice that he doesn't get too close, but just close enough to put on a show for the other guys.

If he wants to play Alpha, I decide that I'll go ahead and play along.

I stand up straight to my full height and use my Alpha voice to say, "I'm not in the mood for games."

He tries to save face in front of the others, but he can't help but step back a bit so I'm a bit less overpowering, though he tries to continue to meet my gaze. The other guys don't have smiles on their faces anymore.

"This here's no game," Pete says. "I wanna know why you keep drivin' through my territory."

I sigh, then I think about Rose, and the pups, Kelly, my broken hand, Kane, Gene, and everything else I need to deal with and decide that I'm truly not in the mood to play 'Alpha games' with the guy.

"First of all," I begin impatiently, "it's not your territory. You're clearly not an Alpha."

At that, Pete's expression changes to something between shock and embarrassment. He's obviously been trying to fool these people for a long time. And the game's over.

"Secondly," I continue, "I don't have time for this bullshit. What kind of a game are you playing here, anyway? You wreck our vehicles, killing two of my warriors in the process, knock us out, and haul us out here to some old rundown hotel, then you turn around and try to patch up my hand."

Pete's eyes go wide, but he doesn't answer.

"And where do you get off sending a young girl in by herself to tend to a strange Alpha? What the hell were you thinking?" I ask, raising my voice a little from irritation.

"It was a test," Pete says, and the other guys nod.

"A test for what?" I ask. "Why would you risk her life for some stupid test? Do you think I'm not pissed at you? If I were any other Alpha, I might take it out on that innocent girl. I'll say it again. You killed my men!"

At that, they all start to back up a bit.

"I could have been anyone," I say. "You have no idea who I am, so you don't know what kind of Alpha I am. What if I were like Alpha Stephen or Alpha Kane?"

With those words, all their eyes went wide. "You know Kane?" asked Pete.

"Yeah, I know him," I say. "And I'm on my way to go rip his throat out, or I was, anyway, until you all stopped me and killed my people."

I open my mouth to say more, but at that moment, the girl who had patched up my hand, Heather, came running into the room, along with Kelly, Trevor, and my other warriors. They freeze in place when they see that Pete is here and look from me to him.

"Are you all right?" asks Kelly.

I nod. "I'm fine," I say. "I was just trying to find out from my new friend Pete here what the fuck his problem is."

Heather giggles at that, and I'd think it was funny too if not for the rest of the situation… and the men we'd lost. I dread having to tell their families. They were both good men with mates and families who will be devastated. Their lives have changed forever, and for what? Some stupid idiot who wants to pretend to be an Alpha.

And somewhere, Rose is sitting in a room, maybe with Kane right there with her, fearing for her life and that of my pup and the others. None of this shit is funny.

I turn and face Pete again. "Listen to me, you idiot," I say, not quite in my Alpha voice but in a voice that makes it clear I've lost every last ounce of patience. "I've got a battle to fight. My mate—" I say it without hesitation and can feel Kelly's shocked reaction, "—my mate is heavy with my child and being held captive by Alpha Kane. I have to get to her, rip him to shreds, save her, and make sure she and the pups are safe!"

Pete backs up and lands in a chair, his shoulders and head dropping at the same time as he puts his hands in his face. He looks up at me. "You have a mate." It was a statement, not a question.

"I do!" I yell at him.

I've never called her that before, and I know she loves the other three Alphas just as much as she loves me, but that's exactly how I feel. When I'm near her, I want nothing more than to be in her arms. When I'm away from her, I want nothing but to return to see her beautiful smile. And when she's in danger, held captive by a monster like Kane, the pain inside my heart feels like a hundred knives ripping me apart from the inside.

Yes, she's my mate. Is it possible the Moon Goddess has given her as a mate to all of us? She's certainly more than worthy of having four strong Alphas at her side.

"I had a mate once," Pete says, almost in a whisper. "I wanted nothing more than to be with her."

As angry as I am with the man, seeing the look in his eyes instantly brings me out of my rage.

"She was like a golden light that brightened up the world," he says. Was....

I lower my head. "I'm so sorry for your loss," I say. I know it doesn't begin to help, but what else can you say in these circumstances?

"Loss," he says, spitting out the word and almost laughing at it. "'Loss' is not enough word for it."

I look up, and the two tall but scrawny men flanking Pete are almost in tears. Clearly, there is a lot of history with this group of rogues, but I really don't have time to dig into it. Everyone just stands quietly for a moment, and I take this time to search my mind for the other Alphas.

I call for them for several moments, but I don't feel their presence at all, so I try to reach Adam back at Gene's castle, but he doesn't answer, either.

"How can we be out of range?" I ask out loud.

One of the scrawny men looks down like he's waiting for Pete to answer, but Pete is clearly somewhere else now, lost in his memories.

"You," I say, nodding toward the scrawny man. "What's your name?"

"Eustace," he says timidly.

"Eustace," I say. "Where the hell are we? We were in range of the castle before, and now I can't reach anyone."

"Oh," says Eustace, "we're a good hund'rd miles from there."

All our heads turn to him. "What?!"

"Yup," he says. "We git a big territory."

"Good Goddess," says Kelly, and I share her sentiment.

I look at her, then back at Eustace. "How did you get us here?" I ask him.

His face brightens up, like he's got some secret weapon he's proud of. "In the van."

"Then that's how you're getting us out of here," I say. I turn to Kelly. "If we pass by, we'll pick them up for a proper burial." I couldn't leave my men out there in the forest alone.

"But—" says Eustace.

I look at him, completely running out of patience again.

"Van's broke," he says, shrugging.

"Oh, good Goddess," Kelly says again. We're really on the same level on the aggravation spectrum.

"What's wrong with it?" I ask.

"Axel broke," he says.

"Do you have parts?"

He thinks about this for a moment. "Yup. I think so," he says.

"Show me," I say, gesturing toward the door. I look at Kelly, and she gives me a nod.

'I'm going to stay and talk to the girl more,' she says in the mind-link. 'I need to find out what's going on here.'

'All right,' I say. 'Just be careful.'

'Always,' she says.

I gesture to Brent and Sean to follow me but instruct Trevor in the mind-link to stay behind with Kelly. I don't want to leave her alone with these people when we don't even know how many of them there are, or how crazy some of them might be out here in this abandoned hotel.

I follow Eustace out to where they keep the vehicle and hope to the Goddess that he really does have the parts we need.

Rose's beautiful smile surfaces in my mind as I walk, and I feel the knives cutting out my heart again.

Nothing is going to stop me from reaching her.

CHAPTER 13: SO MANY QUESTIONS

Tristan

We are nearly to the castle grounds, and I am ready to taste blood. I want to find Alpha Kane and rip his throat out, but then, I hear a voice I don't know in my head that makes me slow down a bit. The other two Alphas that I'm running right alongside also slow down, and I'm wondering if perhaps they are getting the same message.

"Hey, Alphas? I know you don't know me, but my name is Diana, and I'm with Rose."

"Who are you?" I ask immediately.

"Diana!" she says again.

I shake my head. "Yes, I know that, but who are you? What do you want?"

"I want you to know that Rose can't message you right now because Alpha Kane is using some sort of Alpha mind-trick power thing to mess with her, but he isn't doing that to me."

"Where is she?" Reece asks.

Mark chimes in, "Is she okay?"

"She's fine. She's here in the castle with me. But she wanted you to know that Alpha Kane has his sharpshooters ready for whenever you and your forces appear in front of the castle."

"Sharpshooters?" I repeat. "What the actual fuck?"

I stop running, and so do the other two Alphas as we exchange looks of shock and surprise. I pause in my conversation with the mystery woman to tell all of the troops I currently have barreling toward the castle to stop and wait, and I'm also in contact with the men that I have already got fighting at the castle. Why haven't they been affected by these sharpshooters? I don't know the answer, but I'm thankful they haven't been.

"It's abysmal to think that Alpha Kane would actually be using guns!" Mark says.

"He's such an asshole!" Reece agrees. We are all still in our wolf forms, so we are talking to one another using the mind-link, but we are not including our new friend Diana, yet.

But then I ask her, "You said Rose is okay? And she knows we are coming for her?"

"Yes, she knows. She just didn't want you to die trying," the woman tells us.

"Why are you helping her?" Mark asks, and he sounds so rude, I want to punch him, but I don't currently have a hand. "Why would someone who works in Alpha Kane's castle want to help Rose?"

I narrow my eyes at him and say only to him and Reece. "Be nice! She's helping."

He has that look on his face, though. Even as a wolf, I can see it. He's thinking she might be lying to us or otherwise trying to trick us so that we fail.

I tend to see the good in people, though. I tend to assume the best from people. Until they prove me otherwise. Maybe that makes me wrong about people a lot of times, and I end up regretting it when they prove to me that they're not the person I had hoped they were, but I think it's better than always looking over my shoulder or assuming the worst.

"I don't know if she's helping or not! " Mark points out, proving my point about him not trusting others.

"I'm helping her because I like her," Diana says, her tone a little snarky, and I can't blame her. She probably doesn't appreciate her kindness being questioned. "Rose is a nice person, and I would like to see her and her pups get out of here safely. Also, I am hoping that she will agree to take me with her when she leaves, and since Alpha Kane is an awful bastard, I am looking forward to getting as far away from him as fucking possible."

I can see her point, and I'm about to say so when Mr. Grumpy Pants, Mark, says, "Well, I don't know about that. We can't just have a spy running around in our midst, telling our enemies everything."

"A spy?" she echoes, and I can hear that she's offended by his remarks. "Listen, I'm just trying to help. She's in a room on the third floor near the front of the castle. If you want anything else, you know where to find me."

With that, she's gone, and I am left glowering at Mark. "Way to go, you negative Nancy!" I tell him.

"Yeah!" Reece agrees. "Why can't you ever just be nice?"

"Me?" Mark asks, looking all shocked. "You don't think there's a chance she was just telling us what Kane wants us to hear?"

"No! I don't think so!" I tell him. "Why would Kane want her to tell us that he's about to try to shoot us?"

"Because he's not!" Mark replies. "Maybe he's not going to shoot us, he's just saying that so we'll back off. It worked, didn't it? We're not running toward the castle anymore."

I want to tell him where he can shove his theory, but we don't have time for that. "Listen, we know that he has guns, and he's willing to use them, so we need to do something he's not expecting."

"What do you think that would be?" Reece asks.

"I think… we can send in some of our troops from the front, as long as they know what they're up against, and they spend more time zigging and zagging than actually attacking, drawing Kane's own wolves out and using them as shields while we go around and join with our forces that are already fighting, blow through the defenses, and come up on the flanks of the sharpshooters. Maybe they won't know we're there until it's too late."

"That sounds like a solid plan to me," Reece says. "It's too bad we didn't get to ask Diana how many sharpshooters there were or what's going on with them before she left abruptly." He is glaring at Mark, too.

"You guys are never suspicious of anyone, and it's going to bite you in the ass," he says, shaking his wolf head. "All right. Let's do this," he agrees. We send the information we need to our men, and we have several volunteers who are all about distracting the sharpshooters, which is remarkable because it is dangerous.

Then, Mark and Reece break to the north, and I head to the south so that we can go around from opposite sides and sneak up on Kane.

As I am running, I try to connect with Diana again. "Listen, I'm sorry about Alpha Mark," I tell her. "He's just a negative sort of person."

"I don't like him," she says in an angry voice.

"Neither do I sometimes," I admit. "But if you could do us all a favor and get Rose somewhere safe, like at the back side of the castle, near a door where we can get her out, and possibly even hide her from Alpha Kane in case he goes looking for her to use her to make us stop fighting, I would appreciate it, and I'll make sure you are handsomely rewarded."

Diana is quiet for a moment, and I think she might say no, but then she says, "I'll do you one better. I'll bring her right to you."

"But... what about the fighting?" I ask.

She replies, "I can get around that."

CHAPTER 14: SUFFERING A LOSS

KELLY

We certainly don't have time to waste, but there's nothing else to do but try to get the van fixed so we can get on our way. It seems to be the only vehicle these people have, and our utility vehicles were pretty smashed up in the crash.

Especially the one with Ben and Liam.

I know Liam's wife well, and I've hung around with Ben's wife on all the pack's special occasions. Both couples were clearly fated mates, so they're going to be devastated. One look at Pete, and I can imagine what their lives will be like when they find out their mates are gone. He's completely lost, staring out the window like he thinks his mate will appear there magically. It's a horrible fate.

Eli just left with Brent and Sean to work on the van, and Trevor stayed back with me. I'm pretty sure Eli ordered him to do so to protect me, though he must have done so in the mind-link. I can hold my own, and Eli should know that. Sometimes brothers can be such a pain in the ass.

But I stayed behind on purpose to talk to Heather. I'm intrigued with her, and with this place, and I want to know more.

"Tell me about your pack," I say. I know they're not a pack because they're clearly rogues who have attached themselves to a leader who's not an Alpha, but I feel like I should respect Heather by calling them what she's known them to be for as long as she can remember.

She's been staring at Pete like she's hoping he'll snap out of it, but she gives up and turns to me. "You never heard of us, the Stone Creek pack?"

I shake my head. "I'm sorry, no," I say. She looks sad so I add, "Our pack lands are pretty far from here, so we don't travel this way often." I hope she's not offended.

"Oh," she says. "Well, I s'pose since I never heard of y'all either, that makes sense."

I smile.

"Stone Creek is a great place," she says, her eyes lighting up. "We live here in a genuine hotel. Pete says lots o' rich people used to come here and pay good money to be here."

"I bet they did," I say. "It looks like it's a great place."

She nods, but some of the sparkle disappears from her eyes. "Well, the pack was the best till Betsy died."

"Betsy?"

She nods over to Pete, who seems to flinch at the mention of the name but keeps staring out the window, not moving from his spot.

"Pete's mate," she says.

"I see," I say.

"I weren't very old at the time," she says, and now she's looking out the window with a faraway look, too. "But I 'member it all real clear. It used to be a lotta fun here. The whole place had lots of stuff, and we never ran outta anything. My brother and me, we'd run the hallways collectin' stuff."

I nod, and she looks over at Pete. I hear a creak in the floor and sense that Trevor is making himself comfortable in one of the rickety chairs.

"Ever 'thing was old and rundown," Heather continues. "But there was still so much stuff. It's like the people just ran out. Some of the elders... I remember them talking 'bout fixin' the place up, 'bout repaintin' and stuff like that. Pete was happy then. He said we'd do all

66

of it. He said we'd make this place just as special as it were when rich people came here."

She stops talking for a few minutes, then continues, "Then one day, Betsy was at the river. Men came, scary ones, and they grabbed her. Pete and a few other elders, they tried n' stop 'em. Well, they did stop 'em from takin' her but…."

She stops there, and I put my hand on hers. I look over at Pete and see a tear running down his face. He doesn't move to wipe it off.

"Pete didn't never wanna do nothin' again after that," Heather says. "Then we started runnin' outta stuff, and he started to make rules. Rules like who could hunt, who could do the washin', who could get married. Pete didn't want no one havin' no mates no more."

She stops talking now, but I get the picture. I'm amazed that an entire group of shifters could fall into shambles due to the devastating grief of one man, especially since he isn't their Alpha. I don't know a lot about rogues, but I know they do tend to band together. That primal need for a pack never leaves a wolf, even if we leave a real pack. I guess they just needed an Alpha so bad that they clung to Pete no matter what.

"Well, we're here to help now," I say. "We can't stay here now because we need to rescue my friend, Alpha Eli's mate. But I promise we're going to help you."

"You're a nice lady," she says.

I smile and pat her hand, then I look over at Trevor, who has an unreadable expression on his face. Well, I might as well start helping now. "The first thing we need to deal with is these rules…."

ᴴ*ADAM*ᴴ

Shelby and I have searched everywhere we can find in this labyrinth of secret passageways, and we've yet to find this mysterious unlocked door we heard Barbara talking about. Maybe she's just bull-shitting.

I'm thrilled that there aren't any of Kane's warriors to be found anywhere. I am sure Shelby and I are headed to our deaths investigating the tunnels.

Finally, we end up pretty much back where we'd started, finding nothing.

"Well, there's nothing down here," says Shelby. "So where the hell is this door she's talking about?"

"I don't know," I say. "But maybe we should go back upstairs and see if Barbara is still in her room. We might overhear her talking to someone or something."

Shelby nods, and we head out the nearest secret door, which leads to a hallway. Since there are so many hallways in here, and they all look the same after a while, it takes some time for me to get my bearings and figure out that we're close to the library. I remember the plans that the Alphas took, so I head in, gesturing for Shelby to follow, figuring that I'd better clean up things in case Kane's people do infiltrate the castle. The library is empty, and I straighten up the section the Alphas had been working with earlier.

"Odd how there's a door that leads into this room, then another that leads just outside," Shelby says.

I shrug. "Who knows who even built those or what they were for?" I say.

We head out and over to Barbara's room, where we find the door open. The guard is inside, but Barbara doesn't seem to be. The guard looks at me, frightened. "I stopped hearing her inside, and like you said, I came in," he says. "But she's not here. What the hell kind of witch is this woman?"

Shelby chuckles a little. "The worst kind," she says.

I don't want this guard to know about the secret passage, so I excuse him and close the door behind me, then Shelby and I examine all the walls and corners of the room. Sure enough, there's a secret passageway door. Weird that we didn't see Barbara down there a few minutes ago. She must have been sneaky or went a different way.

We follow the hallway in the passageway for a while until we see light, and opening that door, we're out into a hallway again. This one is by the sewing room, so I look inside, hearing a commotion.

And there's Barbara, shouting at the seamstress. I have this weird sense of relief that I found her mixed with the horror of having actually found her, and my brain can't get a handle on those emotions right now, so I don't say a word.

But Shelby does.

"Where the hell have you been?!" she asks her in a sharp tone.

Barbara puts her hand on her hip like she's never been so insulted in her entire life. "I've never been so insulted in my life," she says.

Guess I nailed that one.

'She's not supposed to know we're keeping an eye on her,' I tell Shelby in the mind-link. 'Tell her you were expecting her to measure for clothes.'

"Well, I was expecting you to measure for your new clothes," Shelby says quickly.

I'm impressed because that was really smooth. "You've had us waiting here for a while," Shelby adds.

"Well, I don't know what you're talking about because I've been right here since he brought me here," she says, pointing at me. Of course, that's a lie, because I brought her close to here, but then she was gone, and she didn't come in here then. And we overheard her talking to King Gene.

Regardless, we know where she's at now, so I report in with the Alphas. 'Nothing much happening with Barbara,' I say, happy to have at least one thing to honestly report.

Alpha Tristan answers me. 'Good,' he says. 'But we're a little busy right now. Keep up the good work and give a shout if anything major happens.'

Shelby looks at me funny, and I realize that I'm smiling since the Alpha said I'd done a good job. At least, I think he'd said that.

Barbara looks at me with a knitted brow and goes back to yelling at the seamstress, something about yellow thread. There's not enough room in my brain to waste any of it thinking about what the hell she's talking about, so I take Shelby's hand and lead her outside.

We'll just keep an eye on Barbara from afar.

CHAPTER 15: TIME TO STORM THE CASTLE

MARK

I don't trust this Diana woman, but Tristan and Reece seem okay with her being the one to talk to us for Rose. I have no idea who she is, what her motivation is, or what she's really trying to accomplish.

But the other two are perfectly fine with it, so I'll be out voted. I decide to keep my mouth, and my mind-link, shut for now and just head around the back of the castle so that I can help sneak in and attack Kane's sharpshooters before they can kill any of our warriors.

I am hopeful that this plan of swinging around the back and coming up behind them will help us to get rid of as many of their armed men as possible.

It makes me disgusted to think of Alpha Kane opening fire on a group of wolves. That's just wrong! We are animals, meant to fight with teeth and claws, not to shoot one another like men. If we were incapable of shifting from our human forms to our wolf forms, there wouldn't be anything wrong with it, but we may as well not even be able to shift if they are going to fight like men.

I tear around the back of the castle, gathering many of my best troops with me as I go. It seems quite clear that the battle here is even. We haven't sent our entire force in yet, but now that we are on the scene and have everyone, we can. I want only my best warriors running full speed ahead at those sharpshooters, though.

As we run, I remind them, "These are armed, dangerous lunatics, so be fucking careful! They will shoot you, and take you out, no questions asked. Those bullets are huge, so it's not just gonna be a flesh wound or a little tickle. You zig and zag, stay down, and steer clear. You got it?"

"Yes, Alpha," they all say in unison, and we turn the corner to run behind the castle and come up the other side, narrowing in so that we are close to the brick wall that makes up the exterior of the castle..

When we do that, we are actually behind their forces since my men have managed to keep them at bay while we slid through a break in their line. Sprinting around the corner, I see that Tristan and Reece have managed to do something similar, and all three of us are converging on the line of armed sharpshooters standing in front of the castle, their weapons at the ready.

We slow down as we approach so that they won't hear us coming, spreading out across the back of their line. It isn't until we are close to within twenty paces that one of the commanders sees us. His mouth opens, and he begins to shout something to the others when I barrel into him, knocking him backward onto the ground. The others arrive at their targets at the same time, and we hear the shouts of the men in their human forms as they hit the hard dirt on their backs. Only a couple of the sharpshooters manage to get a shot off, and I don't hear any screams or howls of pain as they do, so I am hopeful that that means that no one was injured.

I don't hesitate to rip the throat out of the man I've got pinned to the ground. Normally, we would take the time to let the humans shift into their wolf forms before we fight, but in this case, these bastards were trying to cheat, so they deserve to die without truly being able to fight us off.

The taste of aluminum fills my mouth as the man's blood squirts between my teeth. As soon as he stops struggling, I let him go and move to the next, but all of the sharpshooters are down, so I charge at the line of wolves that are now in front of us.

A lot of them are panicked as they are now sandwiched between our line that managed to get behind them and the warriors we left out in front. They come flying forward now, having managed to keep from getting shot, and now we are able to tear through Alpha Kane's line from both directions.

Most of Kane's wolves try to run. They attempt to skirt between us and take shelter in the castle, but we are too angry and too quick for that. I grab a large black wolf by the back leg and pull him down, hard. His front paws fly through the dirt as he tries to get away, but I'm not going to let him, and as my teeth tear into the calf muscle on his right leg, my teeth ripping through flesh as he whimpers and continues to claw at the dirt where a stream of blood is now forming.

I use my claws to grab hold of him and yank him back in my direction. Once I have a good grip on him, I sink my razor-sharp claws into his gut and rip down. That gives me the opportunity to let go of him and tear into his neck with my teeth. A moment later, he's done moving. Forever.

I stand up and survey the battlefield. We clearly have them outnumbered now, and everywhere I look, Kane's wolves are either on the ground or groveling, begging for their lives the best they can without actually being able to speak to their attackers since we are all in our wolf form, and they are not in the same pack.

In my head, I hear cries of mercy from wolves who know that we Alphas can hear them even if the others can't, but I ignore them because I am looking for Kane. I do not see him anywhere, and I suppose he must be in the castle then.

"Let's find Kane!" I shout to Reece and Tristan, and since they are done fighting their enemies as well, we take off toward the door.

A guard is standing there in his human form, completely unarmed, and I can tell by his wide eyes and the fresh smell of urine he is petrified. I'm not sure what good he is supposed to do, but he can either cooperate with us or join his friends on the ground.

The three of us stop and growl at him, and within seconds, he yanks the door open for us. "That's what I thought," Tristan says in my head. Behind us, I hear the sound of dozens of wolf paws as our troops storm into the castle. I give the instruction to my troops, "Do not hurt any of the wait staff! No maids, butlers, or otherwise noncombatant pack members, understand?"

A chorus of, "Yes, Alpha!" comes through my head. We move on, spreading out, listening as the wolves behind us head down different hallways and find warriors who are hiding.

I sniff the air and pick up a faint scent I know is Alpha Kane instinctively. I can smell his masculine scent as one Alpha to another.

I take off running in that direction, the other two Alphas with me. This needs to end now. When we find him, Alpha Kane is a dead man.

CHAPTER 16: PLEASE, MOON GODDESS

Eli

Everything is taking too long, including this walk to the garage.

We're all quiet as Brent, Sean, and I follow Eustace so we can get the van, which apparently is the only vehicle on the premises, working again. I don't see any other way to get to Rose as soon as possible. I'm really not much in the mood to help these people because they killed two of my best warriors, but I don't really see a choice.

Besides, it seems to be more Pete's fault that things are the way they are out here than anyone else's. Though I don't blame him for falling apart after the death of his mate—I don't even want to imagine if the same were to happen to Rose—he should have gotten his shit together for the sake of these people.

I can't really place what's going on out here. They're clearly rogues because Pete certainly isn't an Alpha, but they seem to be very close knit as though they're one big family. From everything I'd ever heard about rogues, they simply choose not to be a part of the pack life. That makes them unpredictable... and dangerous. But all these people, except for Pete and his problems, just seem like regular pack members trying to make their lives work for them.

I don't have time to help them do that, though, because I need to get to Rose. If I could, I'd just shift and run there right this instant. But with my hand severely injured, which would be my front paw in wolf form, that's not an option for me. I'd send Kelly and the warriors ahead, but since we're so far away that we can't even engage the mind-link to the other Alphas, running would take far too long and use up too much energy. The rest of them aren't in much better shape physically than I am after the utility vehicle wreck.

"This here's the garage," says Eustace, and his eyes sparkle like the place is his pride and joy.

He has reason to do so because this group of buildings really is impressive. In fact, I think I hear Sean let out a whistle. At one point, this must have been the outbuildings for the resort operations, so I imagine all these buildings held all the vehicles and equipment they needed to maintain the place. I'm hoping that the van is one of those vehicles, and that they'd kept enough spare parts for it lying around so that we can get it up and running quickly.

My optimism, however, disappears like a popped balloon as soon as Eustace opens the garage door. I'm right about the van being a part of the resort because it still has the name of the place, Wooded Acres Resort and Spa, emblazoned across the side. But what I'm not right about is that we can fix it quickly. The van is… a piece of shit. I have no idea how they managed to haul me and my people here only a couple of days ago. There's so much wrong with it, I don't even know where to start.

"Here she is!" says Eustace as though he's announcing the arrival of the Moon Goddess herself. "Ain't she purty?"

I try to wipe the dread and misery off my face. "It's… nice," I say. It's really the only polite thing I can think of at the moment. I certainly have more insight into these people's lives now that I've seen Eustace so excited about this pathetic pile of metal. I give my guys some quick instructions in the mind-link. I don't want them saying anything, and I know neither one has much of a filter.

"Nice?!" Eustace says as though I've insulted the royal family. "This here's the purtiest thing I've seen in a huge long spell."

"It's very pretty," I say, recovering enough to paint a smile on my face. This is the only vehicle I have at my disposal right now that will get me to Rose, so honestly, it is a beautiful sight. I'm going to go ahead and think positive here. "Where are the parts?" I ask.

Eustace frowns for a few seconds then nods his head over toward the other side of the massive—and mostly empty—garage. I follow his gaze and see a pile of what looks like scrap metal near the back of the place. Great.

"Let's do it this way," I say. "Show me what's wrong, then we'll take a look at the parts."

I can feel my guys behind me rolling their eyes. Everything is wrong with this poor vehicle. It deserves to be retired and parked out in a field of wildflowers somewhere where nature can use it as a planter.

Eustace nods and leads me over to the Goddess-forsaken thing and points out how bad the suspension is, and I notice a lot more on my inspection. But I do think that if we just get the suspension figured out, we can take along a few more spare parts and probably make the trip. I hope.

I start giving instructions, and Brent and Sean jump right in. Fortunately, Brent has a bit more experience working on anything with an engine than the rest of us, so he quickly formulates a way to make a few things from the pile of scrap metal work. I'm glad Kelly brought him along, although that might have been Trevor's doing. Either way, we get to work.

"I just need to weld these two together and they should work," Brent says, and Eustace looks at him like he just ate the last cookie in the snack jar.

"What?" I ask Eustace, already knowing the answer.

"Well, the welder ain't so good," he says. "We ain't got much fuel, so we rigged 'er up, but that don't work too well."

"Let me look at it," says Brent. Thank the Goddess he's here. If we get through this, I'm never leaving Rose's side again. Rose... Every time her name passes through my mind, I can see her face and smell her beautiful scent in my mind. And it makes me miss her even more.

We all move over to the welding machine, which barely looks like a piece of functioning equipment. I struggle to keep my composure and am so glad for my guys, who jump in to work on it without hesitation. I'm going to have to find a way to reward them once we get through this. Maybe their families are about to get much bigger houses.

It doesn't take Brent and Sean long to figure out how to make the welding machine work better, and they do, and soon enough, all the pieces are together and fitting onto the van. It actually looks pretty good. All we need to do is make sure the engine runs.

"This looks great, guys," I say. "Let's see how she runs. Let's fuel it up."

Eustace gets that look on his face, and I'm learning to dread it.

"What?" I ask him. It feels like I'm repeating myself.

"Gas ain't nearby," he says.

At this point, I'm actually ready for that, so I quickly reply, "Where is it?"

"It's 'cross Jackson Hill over yonder," he says. "We gotta pump it outta the tanks."

I take a deep breath, my patience wearing thin, and say, "Let's go."

Once again, the guys don't hesitate to get up from where they'd been securing various parts and follow me and Eustace over something that must be Jackson Hill. We arrive there, and sure enough, there's an old gas station, but Eustace is showing his worried face again.

I don't even want to ask, so I just look at him.

"Needs a key," he says.

"Where's the key?" I ask.

"Inside."

I look over at the small gas station, which has been closed for years. "Who has the key to the door?" I ask.

"Pete," Eustace answers.

'Kelly,' I say instantly in the mind-link. 'We need a key to a gas station from Pete.'

She doesn't answer, but I know she's working on it, so I wait a few minutes. 'He's useless,' she says finally. 'Still just staring out the damn window.'

At that, I walk over to the gas station door and give it a quick pound with my shoulder, with all my thoughts about getting to Rose as quickly as I can and saving her and the unborn pups giving me more than enough strength, and the rickety door comes smashing down. I don't even look over at Eustace. I see a panel of keys on the wall and find one marked for the one working pump, which I'm not sure how it could possibly have any gas left, and go over to unlock the bar holding down the nozzle.

Miraculously, something resembling gas comes out, and I fill up all the plastic gas cans I'd found inside. We all carry them back over Jackson Hill to the resort garage and take turns filling up the tank. Luckily, we have a few extras, so we load those into the back of the van.

Rose feels so close now. All I have to do is get to her.

I climb into the driver's seat and spot a key already in the ignition. I close my eyes for a few moments, saying a silent prayer to the Moon Goddess that she will lead me there to Rose and the pups and that when I get there, they will all be unharmed.

I take one last deep breath and turn the key.

CHAPTER 17: LIGHT AT THE END OF THE TUNNEL

I follow along with Diana as she leads me down a dark hall, and it makes me nervous. It reminds me of the tunnels the others found in the walls of King Gene's castle. It reminds me that I was dragged through a secret passage to get me out of the castle. I have vague memories of being wrapped in a sheet and dragged through the darkness. My feet are still bruised from it. I believe it was Barbara who did that to me, but I'm not sure.

As I rush behind the maid, my abdomen begins to hurt, and I have to slow down. "Diana!" I shout to her. "Where are we going? And can we slow down?"

"This passage comes out in the woods on the far east side of the castle," she explains to me. "I'm trying to get you away from Kane. I know that he will do whatever he can to keep your Alphas from attacking him. If that means using you as some sort of a human shield, he'll do it. We need to make sure he can't find you when he comes looking for you."

Everything she is saying makes perfect sense. It's just, the further I walk, the more my stomach hurts. I can ignore the chaffing from my thighs rubbing together, the pain in my lower back from carrying all of these babies, and the agony in my head from the drugs they gave me to knock me out, but I can't handle these cramps I'm having in my abdomen.

Ahead of us, I can see a crack of light that looks like it's the frame of a door, so I keep going. All I want, more than anything in this world, is to be safe in a soft bed with all four of my men around me.

Now that I can see the light at the end of the tunnel, that doesn't seem as impossible as it did a few minutes ago.

Reece

We are in the castle now, and our warriors are doing a great job of finding and destroying Alpha Kane's men, but we are not after just any warrior.

No. Alpha Tristan, Alpha Mark, and I are on the prowl for the big man himself. We need to find the Alpha who lives here and destroy him.

And then, we need to find Rose.

I know that the woman she's with, Diana, is trustworthy. I could hear it in her voice. It seems obvious to me that Alpha Mark doesn't think she has Rose's best interest at heart, but he tends to be negative and overreact to everything.

I can't think about that now as I settle my nose on Alpha Kane's scent. At first, I could only pick up traces of him, probably because this is his home, and his smell is everywhere. But as we head down a particular hallway, I smell him more than I had before.

We pick up speed, and since the hallways are so narrow, I almost run into Tristan. I can imagine the two of us getting wedged in here and Mark having to push through the wedge we'd create and dislodge us.

The scent leads us to a room, but when I stop outside of the closed door, I realize it's not just Alpha Kane's scent I'm smelling so strongly here.

It's also Rose's.

Just a hint of her familiar scent has my stomach tightening and my breath becoming shallow. I miss her so badly. I would love to wrap my arms around her, to kiss her, to hold her close. I need to see her with my own eyes and make sure she's safe.

Tristan kicks the door in, and when he does, we see Alpha Kane standing in the middle of a bedroom in his human form with a sharp blade in his hand, but he's not alone.

He has a woman wrapped in a sheet in his arms, her head covered by the white cloth. She is crying, and he has the look in his eyes that tells me he has lost his last marble.

"Don't come any closer!" he shouts. "If you do, I'll kill her. I'll kill your precious breeder!"

I exchange a quick glance with Mark and Tristan as we all pause in our places. Is Alpha Kane trying to trick us into believing the woman he's holding beneath the sheet is Rose?

I can smell her here. She's definitely been in this room for a while and recently. Looking at the sheet he has wrapped around the woman, I notice that the bottom is dirty, and I think there's a good chance that it's the sheet from Rose's bed at Alpha King Gene's castle. It smells a lot like her, and I even smell traces of us on it, which is possible if her sheets hadn't been changed since the last time we were in her room. I smell Kelly, Shelby, and Adam as well.

But this woman? She sounds nothing like Rose. Nor is she big enough to be Rose right now, not unless she's already had our pups, and I do not smell anything in this room to indicate that the babies have been born. And Diana didn't mention it. No, this crying woman isn't Rose.

I do feel sorry for her, though, and I hope she doesn't get hurt, but right now, my biggest focus is on taking out Kane and then finding Rose.

Using the mind-link, I say, 'That's not her. Let that woman go.'

"What?" Kane questions aloud. "What do you mean this isn't her?

Of course it is. You don't recognize the scent of your own woman? Maybe that's because she's got the seed of so many men on her body. Maybe even including mine." He grins at us mischievously, and I want to kill him. Who the fuck does he think he is?

'I'm not wasting another second on this bullshit,' Tristan says to Mark and me. 'Let's take him out.'

'We can't hurt that woman, though,' Mark says. 'She's innocent.'

'We don't know that!' Tristan barks back. 'She's obviously one of his people.'

I don't want to argue. I just want to take out Kane. For all we know, there's a trap door or a secret passage here, and he could disappear on us again.

We can't let that happen. I hope the innocent lady doesn't get hurt either, but if she does... she does.

'You go left, Tristan,' I say. 'I'll go right. Mark, you try to get that woman away from him before he hurts her. If we move quickly enough, he shouldn't have time to hurt her.'

'But...' Mark begins.

Tristan cuts him off, though. 'One, two... three!'

I break to the right as Tristan goes left. Mark misses a beat because he's too busy stewing, but then he lunges right at Kane, attempting to hit him before he can cut the woman.

Kane was bluffing because he doesn't try to cut the woman. Instead, he pushes her toward Tristan, screams like a little girl, and takes several steps backward, not even trying to shift.

He can't get away from us, and as my teeth sink into his soft, warm flesh, he screams louder, and I bite harder.

His blood is warm and salty, and I swallow it down, so glad to finally end him and this conflict.

CHAPTER 18: ROSE NEEDS US NOW!

Kelly

"Are you there?" asks Heather.

I've just started talking to Eli in the mind-link, so I must have sort of drifted off in the middle of my conversation with Heather. But Eli has good news, so I need to focus.

'This piece of shit just started,' he's saying. 'Hurry up and get to the garage, and let's get the hell out of here before it changes its mind.'

"I need to find the garage," I tell Heather.

She nods. All I have to do is gesture toward the door, and Trevor gets the picture. We're more than ready to get out of here.

"We need to hurry," I tell both of them.

We leave Pete behind, just sitting in the room. He's stopped staring out the window finally, but now he's just staring at the ceiling. No wonder things don't get done around here.

Heather takes my haste seriously and practically runs toward what I'm hoping is the garage. I don't know if there's more than one, so I hope wherever she's leading us is where Eli is. It seems to take forever, but finally we reach a group of buildings dotted around an area that's completely paved.

And I hear a car.

A van, to be precise, and soon after that, I see the vehicle pulling out of one of the garages with Eli behind the wheel, smiling smugly but also looking incredibly impatient. And I see clearly why he'd called it a piece of shit. It was apparently once a shuttle of some kind with lots of seats like a bus, and it has the name of the resort, which was apparently Wooded Acres Resort and Spa, plastered all over the side of it in faded letters. There's more rust than paint, and it honestly looks like it's held together with glue and duct tape. Even if I ignore its looks, the sputtering of the engine can't be good.

But I hop inside anyway, followed by Trevor. Heather jumps in and climbs next to me in the middle seat as if we're going for a Sunday drive in the country. I suppose we are.

"Won't your parents get worried about you?" I ask. "We'll be gone a very long time."

She shrugs. "Ain't never been worried before," she says, and now I worry about what kind of parents this young lady has.

"Maybe you should've brought some of your stuff," I say, knowing it's too late for that anyway because Eli is already driving down the road.

Heather shrugs again and says, "Ain't nothin' I need."

I nod because none of us have anything with us; I'm not even going to ask what they did with the stuff on our utility vehicles. I turn around and smile at Brent and Sean, who are sitting in the back seat along with that Eustace person who had taken them to fix this thing earlier. He smiles back with brown teeth, and I turn back around to face the front and look at Eli.

"Do we even have gas?" I ask. I can't imagine there being anyplace to get gas for this thing way out here.

"There was a gas station," he says. "Surprisingly with lots of gas in the tank."

"Is it still any good?" I ask. "It's probably been decades since it's been refilled." Heather looks at me a little funny, and I realize I'm probably insulting her, so I switch to the mind-link. 'And are you sure this piece of shit isn't going to get us stranded?'

'It doesn't sound great, or look great, but it's actually pretty solid,' he says, also in the mind-link.

'Are we going the right way?' I ask.

'Yes,' he says. 'Eustace says this old road hits Highway 30, and that heads straight to Kane's territory.'

I look forward at the road we're on, or at least what's left of it. Decades of neglect and Mother Nature's attempts to reclaim it are showing with the wide cracks and overgrowth. In some places, I can barely see the road since it looks like a pile of weeds. 'This is an old road alright,' I say.

'At least we're finally headed in the right direction,' he says. I can only see the side of his head, but I can make out the determined look on my brother's face. I know that all he's thinking about is getting to Rose.

I'm not in a hurry to drive up into the middle of a war, but I can hold my own in battle, and I think it'll be better for Rose to have me there with her in case the babies start coming. Not that I'm any kind of an expert, but I can imagine how all these Alphas might start panicking when the babies are being delivered, and I think Rose needs a strong woman's hand to hold onto.

I can't even imagine having four pups at the same time. Well, I can sort of imagine, but I've never even had a single pup before, so I don't have any motherhood experience to draw from. While guarding Rose back at the castle, I'd read plenty of her books about childbirth while she was asleep, and that is scary stuff.

Even after the babies are born, there's so much to worry about— whether they're eating right, whether they're growing right, whether you're doing something wrong that's going to mess them up for life. I'm glad she has all four Alphas as a support system. It's going to be a wild ride.

Speaking of which, I jerk suddenly as the bus lurches, and I nearly fall out of my seat. Eli is cursing endlessly, and I want to wrap my hands around Heather's ears, but she just sits there and smiles. I guess she's used to it with Pete and the like.

"What is it?" I ask as Eli slows the van to a stop.

"Looks like we blew a tire," he says, thankfully stopping the cursing because he's just caught sight of Heather in the rear view mirror.

We all exit the van and walk around to the driver's side, which has a flat tire in the rear. "I hope we have a spare," I say.

"Yup," says Eustace, still smiling at me and holding his gaze on my chest for a tad too long.

I take Heather's hand and lead her around to the other side of the van. There's a nice shady tree on the side of the road, so we head over there to sit down out of the sun while Eli and the others deal with the tire. Sure enough, I see them digging out a spare and a pretty sturdy looking jack, so I exhale. Being stranded out here would be the worst, but I'm confident they'll get it fixed. I start to wonder about the trip back and how far we'll have to drive before we can use the mind-link again to talk to the other Alphas, and hopefully Rose, too.

"Are you Eustace's mate?" Heather suddenly asks.

I'm jolted out of my thoughts. "What?" I say. I'm not sure I heard her right.

"Eustace," she says. "Are ya mates?"

I shake my head and wish there were some way I could do so more ferociously. "No!" I say. "What makes you ask that?"

"I seen the way he's been lookin' at ya is all," she says. "Thought maybe you felt a mate pull."

"Oh, Goddess, no," I say, then I wonder if maybe I'm offending her again. I'm sure Eustace will make a great mate... for someone who's not me. "I mean, I'm sure he's a nice man, but no, there's nothing there."

"Oh," she says, looking at the ground and plucking some weeds from among the grass.

I look at her, fascinated, while she wraps the stem of the weed around its top, which has a stiff looking seed pod there, and with a flick of her finger, she shoots the pod into the air.

"How did you do that?" I ask her.

She smiles and picks another weed stem, handing it to me, then gets her own and demonstrates. I manage to get mine to flick several feet. Pretty soon, we're both giggling and flicking weeds like schoolgirls.

"I wish you were his mate," she says when the giggles subsided a bit. "Then you could join my pack."

I'm not sure what to say to her. I want to tell her that she's not in a pack, and never has been, but I can tell by the earnest look on her face that she's not ready to hear that yet. I'm going to tell her, but not now. Maybe Rose can help me break it to her when we get back.

"I guess the Moon Goddess doesn't have that in her plans," I say, finally thinking of something. "But she brought me to meet you, so I think she meant us to be friends."

"Really?" she says.

"Yes," I say, nodding. "I think we could be good friends."

"I'd like that," she says.

I stand up as I see the men boarding the bus again and waving us over. Heather has a new spring in her step, and I'm smiling a bit, relieved that the tire is fixed. And I guess I've made another friend. All I have to do now is get back to my other friend before her babies are born.

I can sense that Rose really needs us there, and fast.

CHAPTER 19: THOSE STUPID ALPHAS DID THIS TO ME!

Rose

"Diana!" I have to shout out to her as she pushes through the door at the end of the tunnel, and I can see a flight of stairs leading out to the forest. "I need to rest!"

"We're almost there," she tells me, but I'm breathing so hard, I don't know how I will make it up the stairs. And if there are any kind of enemies lurking about up there, well, they may as well just kill me now and save me the horror of having to drag my massive pregnant lady body up those stairs.

"Come on!" Diana says, sounding a bit encouraging but mostly irritated. "You can do it!"

"I really don't think I can!" I can barely get the words out before a horrible pain hits me in the side. I double over, screeching, and Diana comes running back to me.

"What is it?" she asks, and I can hear the fear in her voice.

"The babies," I say, suddenly feeling like I need to lay down so that I can start pushing or something. "I believe my children have picked this most inconvenient time to make their appearance in the world." As another contraction hits, I think about everything I've read. Wasn't

I supposed to be counting? Mark was going to be the one to count! He was supposed to do that while Tristan said soothing things, and Reece feeds me ice chips.

Eli was supposed to rub my feet....

Nothing is going as planned!

"Where is Dr. Panthergash?" I snarl as Diana stands near me, looking helpless.

"Your doctor's name is Dr. Panthergash?" she asks me.

I look up into her eyes and shout back, "I don't have any fucking idea what my doctor's name is!"

Her gaze widens as I have alarmed her, and she says, "Okay, sorry. We have a pack healer, but I doubt you're going to want him to help you."

"No!" I yell at her, and then I start to cry. "I'm sorry. It's not your fault. You're lovely, Diana. It's just... this really hurts, and I have no idea where my men are!"

"Well, I told them I'd get you out of the castle," she says. "I can check with them, but one way or another, you're going to have to get out of this tunnel, and there's a good chance that, if your Alphas are storming the castle, the others who know about this tunnel are going to come flying down it soon. So..."

My eyes go to the stairs and I can't help but curse beneath my breath. I don't want to get run over by fleeing people from the castle, but those stairs look so daunting. They're steep, and there has to be at least twenty of them.

I think I hear a noise behind me and have to wonder if that's someone coming through the tunnel. Reluctantly, I head toward the stairs, but as my foot comes down on the first one, another contraction hits, and I know I can't go any higher. I cry out in agony and put both feet back on the ground before the step. That's an option for now, but if I'd already been five or ten steps up, I might've fallen.

I sink to the ground, my tears falling harder as I sob, "I can't do it!"

"Sure you can!" Diana says, tugging on my arm.

I jerk away from her. "No, I can't! I can't do it! You should just leave me here and save yourself!"

"Don't be stupid!" Diana says. "I'm not leaving you here. Just… let me check with the Alphas. Maybe they'll know what to do. I would carry you, but I don't think I can lift you with all of those pups."

"No, you couldn't. No one can! I weigh more than a fucking mountain! Those stupid Alphas did this to me! Made me all fat and unmovable! I hate them!" I don't hate them, though. I love them. I do wish they were here to help–and also so that I could slap them senseless.

I continue to sit on the ground crying, screaming with every contraction as Diana stands between me and a slow trickle of wolves that comes through the tunnel. They all look at me funny, but none of them attempts to bite me or anything as they head up the stairs.

My only thoughts are that I want these babies out of me so that I can move my body again. That and where the hell are my Alphas?

TRISTAN

ALPHA KANE IS DEAD. We all had a chance to chomp into him before he died, and now, his body lies bleeding all over the carpet in one of his rooms. It's satisfying, knowing we have vanquished one of our enemies. Stephen isn't much of a threat compared to Kane, so hopefully, now, we can go back to dealing with the most important matters at hand–Rose and the pups.

Thoughts of her enter my mind as I turn to the others. 'We need to find Rose,' I remind them.

'Why don't you ask your little friend Danish or whatever the fuck her name is,' Mark snarls. 'I'm sure she's taking excellent care of her.'

'It's like you're fucking jealous of the woman who is trying to get Rose away from the fighting,' Reece says, shaking his head.

'I think we should call for a transport vehicle before we even find her,' I say. 'We need to get her out of here, away from the threat of Kane's troops that might rally yet, even though he's dead. Mark, how far is it to your territory from here?'

'Not too far,' he says, still angry. 'Maybe twenty minutes by transport.'

'Can you call for a vehicle?' I ask him. 'Let's take her there. I think, if she's about to have the babies, we should have time, and that will give her a chance to be more comfortable away from this nasty place.' I didn't even like being in Kane's castle, and I wasn't about to pop some other people out of my body.

'Fine,' he says. 'I'll get the transport on the way and alert the healers.'

'We should see if we can get Dr. Penderghan to meet us there as well,' Reece suggests, and I like that idea.

While those two are working on that, I begin to try to connect with this Diana person, but before I can even start to formulate a message to her, I hear her voice in my head. 'Hey! Where are you guys? Rose is going into labor!'

'Shit,' I mutter. 'In the castle. Where are you?' Before she answers, I realize that I should be able to talk to Rose directly now since Kane is dead.

'We are at the bottom of the stairs that leads out through the tunnel.' She tells me quickly how to find the tunnel, and I signal for the other two to follow me. We head down the hallway, and before long, I see the doorway she's talking about. It's in the wall, the way that the other secret passages back in Gene's castle were situated. And a few wolves and a couple of people in their human forms are going through it.

We don't hesitate to blaze right through, running at full speed. We dodge around a couple of kids and almost knock an older wolf over, but before long, we are ahead of the pack. While I'm running, I try to call Rose. I just want to hear her voice.

'Don't worry, little flower,' I tell her. 'We are coming to save you!'

'Where the fuck are you?' she screams. 'I hate all of you, you stupid bastards! Why did you have to put these giant babies in me?'

'Well, in fairness, they were a lot smaller going in,' I tease, and when she screams a string of obscenities at me, I realize that probably wasn't the smartest thing I could've said to her.

But then I see her–sitting on the ground, crying, clearly in pain– and as beautiful as ever. As we run toward her as fast as we can, all I can think about is how lucky I am that she is mine–she loves me, and I love her, and maybe she loves these other guys, too, but that woman is mine, and I will take care of her. No matter what.

CHAPTER 20: THE MOON GODDESS BROUGHT HER TO YOU

Eli

My heart aches so bad I can barely concentrate on the road ahead of me, but I know it's the only way I'm getting to Rose. It feels like I should just jump out and shift, and it'll go faster, but I know that's not possible right now with my hand injury.

In fact, it's hard to even steer the van with the way my hand is wrapped up right now. I just have to hope this piece of shit gets me there. If it does, I'm going to have every mechanic in my pack work on this thing to restore it to completely brand-new condition, then I'm going to keep it forever. I'll pay Pete, or whoever owns it in his group of rogues, good money.

It'll be my lucky van.

"How are you holding up?" Kelly's voice invades my thoughts and almost makes me turn the wheel in surprise. We're going fairly fast, so I'm glad I don't.

"I don't know," I say. "I just need to get there."

She nods. "We all do," she says. "And we will."

"I know, but that doesn't make the 'getting there' any easier," I say.

"I've never been on this road," she says, looking ahead, maybe trying to change the subject.

We've hit the highway now so it's faster going, thank the Goddess, and that means we're getting closer to a place where I can reach everyone in the mind-link. Not knowing has been a nightmare that's almost worse than having Rose kidnapped in the first place. Well, not really of course, but this whole idea of not knowing where she's at gives me an unbearable level of anxiety that feels like rocks in my stomach.

I just need to know she's okay. She has to be okay.

"She's going to be okay," says Kelly as though she's reading my mind.

"I keep telling myself that," I say. "But the worrying is unbearable. I mean, it's hard enough on a woman, isn't it, to have one baby? She's having four. And on top of that, she's kidnapped, right when she's practically ready to have the babies, all alone without us in some strange castle with some maniac Alpha who's using her for... who knows what! That's stress on top of stress on top of stress. Is she really going to be okay?"

I take my eyes off the road for a second to look at Kelly, and the look on her face is unreadable. She's trying to be strong for me. Sisters can be annoying, but boy do I need her right now.

"Watch the road," she says.

Annoying again. It almost makes me laugh.

"Rose is a very strong woman," she says. "Look at all she's been through in her life. Her parents treated her like garbage and made her work her ass off for them. She had to do some of the worst jobs possible back in her home pack... and look at her. She's strong, resilient. She was supposed to come be a breeder. Do you know how terrifying that is to a young woman? But she got on that train and did everything she was supposed to do to make that happen. Now, I'm sure the Moon Goddess played a huge role in that. But still, it was Rose's strength that got her to that point. I have a lot of faith that she will be alright, and so will the pups."

I nod, tears beginning to stream down my eyes.

"Now, don't start that," she says, reaching into her pocket to pull out a tissue. I can't believe she has a tissue in the middle of nowhere.

"You won't be able to see the road." She giggled and I tried to smile. "There we go. It's really going to be okay. Do you think the Moon Goddess would go through all the trouble to make Rose be such a strong woman, then have her come to you as your mate, and probably the mate of the others too, and get pregnant with your pup and the others, only to have something happen to her?"

She has a point.

"Of course not," she says, answering her own question. "This," she says as she gestures around the van and at the road in front of us, "was all meant to be."

There's a strength in her voice, a determination that everything is going to be okay, and it sparks something inside me. She's right. The Moon Goddess brought the most perfect woman in the world to me for a reason. She's going to be okay. We're going to be okay.

"Now, I'm going to go talk to my new friend, Heather," she says, patting me on the shoulder. "There's no crying and driving, so focus."

"I'm not crying," I say, as tears are still streaming down my cheeks.

"Mmhmm," she says and walks back to sit by Heather.

I focus back on the road and the long drive ahead. I have hope in my heart even through all the pain. I'm going to get to her. I push on the gas a little and speed up, knowing I'm getting closer.

ADAM

'Does anyone there have a watch?' asks Shelby in the mind-link while flipping through pages.

The Alphas have brought us all into a single mind-link so we can consult all Rose's childbirth books while they rush her to Alpha Mark's pack hospital, which is the closest one to Alpha Kane's castle. Well, I guess it's not his castle anymore since he's dead. Thank the Goddess.

'Why do we need that?' asks Alpha Tristan.

Shelby looks up at me, exasperated, as if I'm the one who just asked the question. Even I know that a woman has to time contractions, but I really don't blame the Alphas for being in panic mode right now, because Rose is already in labor.

Instead of yelling at him and calling him an idiot, which she would probably do to me, she calmly says, 'We need to time her contractions. Now, are you sure her water didn't break?'

'No,' answers Alpha Reece, who somehow seems to be the calmest of all of them and probably still remembers about timing contractions. 'But I do have a watch. I'm supposed to time the minutes between them, right?'

'Yes,' Shelby answers with composure. When did my wife become able to be so relaxed in a crisis? I'm pretty impressed with her right now, and it's frankly turning me on. 'The next time she has one, time the distance between them. And if her water does break, let me know.'

Dr. Penderghan came into the room we're in, which is right across from where Barbara is currently arguing with Gene, since I need to keep an eye on her. "What's the news?" the doctor asks. The Alphas had wanted her to meet them at Alpha Mark's castle, but Dr. Penderghan has a very seriously ill patient here and wasn't willing to leave when she knows Alpha Mark's healers can handle this.

'Alphas, I have Dr. Penderghan with us. Add her in,' Shelby says.

They continue to have a conversation about minutes and timing and water or no water, and the doctor talks directly with Rose for a bit, which is frankly a relief instead of having the Alphas try to interpret for her. I don't know why they didn't do that in the first place.

They're not too far away from Alpha Mark's place, so hopefully Rose will be in a hospital bed with the healer there very soon.

In the meantime, Barbara's argument with Gene is getting louder. I swear, all that woman does is argue.

"What the fuck do you mean?" yells Gene. He's pretty good at arguing himself. I think the two of them actually enjoy it and would be bored if there wasn't any arguing. "I've spent a fortune on your fucking clothes and you're still not happy?"

"The future Luna of this pack cannot go about in rags!" Barbara says. "Never mind. I'll deal with this myself!" She walks off in a huff, and Gene comes out of the room and stares at me through the open door, then he barges into this room.

"What's going on in here?" he asks. "Doctor? Is someone sick?"

We hadn't told him what was going on at all. He doesn't know that Alpha Kane is dead, or that Rose has been rescued, or that the pups are about to be born. The less he knows about all this, the better. The Alphas wanted it that way.

"Oh, yes," says Shelby, and she coughs and pounds on her chest.

The doctor, being wonderful, picks up on it instantly and pretends to be examining her. "I definitely think you need bed rest," she says.

Gene walks over and looks at her. "What's wrong with her?" he asks.

"She has… she has a tussis russis virus," the doctor says. It sounds like something made up, but I nod anyway. "And I'm trying to examine this patient, Your Majesty, if I may?" she added.

Gene looks at her. "Oh, yes. Carry on," he says. "But get this sick woman out of my wing. We can't have sick women in my wing!"

"Right away, Your Majesty," I say, and thankfully Gene walks off, muttering to himself about women and sickness and clothes.

The doctor and Shelby go back to their discussion with the Alphas, and now I have to go catch up to find Barbara and find out where the hell she went. Once again, I have one job, and I'd better get it right.

I'll leave the childbirth thing to the experts.

CHAPTER 21: IT'S A TRAVESTY

Rose

"I'm going to die!" I scream as Tristan and Mark lift me in their human forms to carry me up the stairs. Mark has my upper body, and Tristan has my lower body, and I feel like my middle is going to collapse on me as they hoist me up. I want to shout at Reece to support me there, but I don't know where the fuck he went, and my contractions hurt so fucking bad, if I did see him, I'd probably punch him.

"It's okay, gorgeous," Mark says. "We aren't going to let you die."

"Go to hell, you asshole!" I shout, turning my head to try to look at him. The second my eyes settle on his blue ones, wide with concern, I begin to cry. "I'm so sorry, Mark!" I blubber. "I didn't mean that. I love you so much!"

"It's all right, baby," he says softly. "I know you didn't mean it. I love you, too."

Another contraction hits me, and before I can think about how much I love him and how much I've missed him, a stream of obscenities comes flying out of my mouth, and it's worse than my dad when his favorite sports team is losing.

"Wow," Tristan mumbles. "Mark, I think our girl here is part sailor."

"Fuck off, Tristan, you big piece of shit!" I yell, and then I see him cringe, and immediately, I feel terrible. "I'm so sorry!" are the next words out of my mouth, but it won't take it back.

"I know you didn't mean it," he says, but I think I still see some sadness in his eyes.

Eventually, we reach the top of the steps, and I insist that they put me back down. "Can the vehicle make it through the forest?' I ask. "Because if I have to walk, I'm going to fucking lose my mind!"

"Yes, it can," Reece assures me, coming out from between the trees. All three of them are just wearing short shorts that someone must've handed to them, so ordinarily, I would be checking out their gorgeous bodies, but right now, all I can think about is how they tricked me with those magnificent physiques by making me think they were so hot and so perfect, and they really just wanted to torture me and get me knocked up with these squirmy, diabolical babies.

My babies... the sweetest children in the whole world!

And now I am crying again!

I hear the sound of an engine approaching, and I am praying that it is an ambulance of some sort, equipped with a doctor who can give me an epidural, the little piece of heaven I read about in all of those baby books, or that they will just knock me out completely, and when I wake up, I'll have four beautiful, well behaved babies, my old body back, and feel like a million bucks.

It is not an ambulance I see through my tears winding between the trees, though. It's just a regular black van, and I have a feeling it's not going to be that comfortable, especially if we have to drive over uneven ground to get to wherever the hell we're going. I try not to groan again as Tristan and Mark lead me over. Reece opens the doors, and I do see a woman in the back who looks a lot like a midwife, but she's not Dr. Peepeegash, so it makes me nervous. What if she doesn't know what she's doing? I hate the fact that I'm not going to have my own doctor here.

"Hi, Miss Rose," the older woman says. "I'm Dr. Travesty. I'll be here to help you with the babies every step of the way!"

I am lifted inside of the van and placed down on some blankets, but her name has just hit me. "I'm sorry–what the hell is your name?" I ask her.

She grins at me sheepishly. "Now, now, don't let my name fool you. I assure you, I am perfectly capable of–"

"Dr. Travesty?" I ask as Reece closes the doors. Then, the three Alphas and Diana get into the van and we start on our way over the bumpy forest floor, headed toward Mark's castle. I haven't even gotten a chance to see much of the men since they told me the plan and then began to help me up the stairs, so it's not like Mark or anyone else has told me much about her.

I'm afraid I don't trust her.

"Yes, yes, that's right," she says as she begins to examine me with a stethoscope. "Dr. Mary Travesty."

"As in Bloody Mary?"

She chuckles as she listens to my stomach. I don't know what the fuck she thinks she's doing. That stethoscope isn't going to get these babies out of me. "No, not Bloody Mary, darling. Just Mary."

I have my own opinion about that. I don't like this. Not one bit. But what am I going to do? I requested Dr. Pentupgas be sent to the castle, but the Alphas said she was too busy with some elderly sick patient, so Dr. Travesty is going to have to do.

Why does Mark have a healer named Dr. Travesty?

As another contraction hits hard, I can't help but scream. I grab for something to squeeze, anything, and end up with Mark's hand. He is screaming, too, and when Tristan laughs, Mark punches him in the nose. Red blood begins to trickle down his chin, and now Dr. Travesty is trying to wipe it up and ends up with blood on her hands.

Yeah, it's a travesty all right.

"How long until we get to the castle?" I ask.

"Not long now. Only about twenty minutes," Dr. Travesty says, and I try not to cry louder. This is taking forever. I am back to my old idea that I'm not gonna make it.

"Can I have an epidural?" I ask her.

The doctor laughs louder this time. "Heavens, no, dear. I can't give you an epidural in a moving van. You might get your spinal cord nicked and end up paralyzed! No, we'll evaluate the situation when we get to the castle, and if there's time, we may give you an epidural then."

"If there's time?" I ask her, staring at her like she just said I'm sentenced to death in five minutes.

"Well, if the babies are already crowning, there's no point in–"

I reach over and grab Dr. Travesty by the collar. "You listen to me, bitch, and you listen good. I don't care if the first fucking baby is already in college when we get there, as long as I have a baby shoved up my who-ha, you're giving me an epidural, you hear me, you fucking bitch?!?"

Her mouth drops open, and Tristan pries my hands off of her, and I can tell I've scared the shit out of the doctor who is supposed to keep me and the babies safe. I would feel bad about it if another contraction didn't make me want to scream.

Yep, I'm gonna die.

CHAPTER 22: I'M ALMOST THERE, BABY

Eli

'Eli, you fucking asshole! Where are you?!'

The voice comes screaming into my mind, and instantly, my heart races, and my wolf inside howls in pure joy. It takes a minute for me to process it, though. Did Rose just call me an asshole?

'Oh, my Goddess,' I say back. 'Where are you, baby? Are you okay?'

'No!' she screams at me. 'I am most definitely not okay! Why aren't you here? What the fuck could you possibly have to do that's more important than being here, you selfish jerk!'

I don't know what to say to answer that, and I'm completely confused. This voice sounds like Rose, and my wolf feels her presence, but why is she talking to me like that? She's never done that before, ever.

'Oh, my Goddess,' she says next. 'I'm so sorry!'

'It's okay, baby,' I say, happy that I've got my Rose back as I know her. 'Where are you? What's happening?'

'I'm... I'm in a van, and it's the suckiest, most piece of shit van in the world....'

I smile at that, considering the vehicle I'm currently driving.

'And Dr. Travesty isn't giving me an epi—ahhh!' She finishes in one of the most blood-curdling screams I've ever heard, and I've been through many war battles.

'Baby?!' I say, and that knot is back in my stomach. What the hell are they doing to Rose? It sounds like some sort of torture. I swear, when I get my hands on Kane, I'm ripping him to shreds. And who the hell is Dr. Travesty? Is it some new name for Dr. Penderghan? I hope and pray to the Moon Goddess that Rose is in the hands of that friendly and competent doctor, but right now, I have no idea.

'I'm okay,' she says then. 'Just another contraction.'

"Contraction?!" I scream it out loud without meaning too, and everyone in the van hears me.

"Oh, my Goddess," says Kelly. "Are you talking to Rose? Is she in labor?"

All I can do to answer is nod.

"Bring me in!" Kelly hollers, and I bring her into the mind-link.

'All I want to do is get out of this... ahhhh!' says Rose with another horrible scream. The sound of it makes me want to kill whoever is doing it to her and strangely, at the same time, I feel like I need to run far, far away. But I won't. I'm going to get to her. She's having my baby! And it's happening right now by the sound of it!

'Breathe,' Kelly says in a calm, soothing voice. Voice works a little differently in the mind-link than in person, but it does allow us to convey emotion as well as words, so I think the soothing sounds are helping.

But only for a minute.

'You miserable fucking asshole!' screams Rose. 'Why did you fucking do this to me?!' It's followed quickly by, 'Oh, no! I'm so sorry. Where are you?'

Kelly chuckles behind me. 'Don't apologize,' she says. 'I've been around him forever, and sometimes I'd agree with that name.'

I ignore her teasing because I have more important things to worry about right now. 'I'm on the road headed to you, baby,' I say. 'We're almost at Kane's castle, and I'll be there soon!'

'No!' she yells back at me.

'What do you mean, no?' I ask. 'Don't you want me there?' I'm confused and a little hurt for a moment. Then I think about it, and remember how painful childbirth must be, so Rose probably isn't herself right now. But still, does she not even want me there?'

'I'm not there!' she says. That's right. She'd said she was in a van.

'Where are you?' I ask.

'I'm... ahhhh!'

'Breathe through it,' says Kelly softly. 'Breathe through it.'

'Eli?!' says Tristan.

'Yes, I'm on my way,' I say.

'We just realized that she must be talking to you because she stopped cursing like a sailor at us!' he says.

'You're all there?'

'Yes,' he says. 'We're taking her to Mark's pack since that's the closest. His healer, Dr. Travesty, is with her. We'll be there in a couple of minutes.'

So that means I have to change course a bit. I'm glad she's not going to have our babies in Kane's castle, but now I'll have a little farther to drive to get to her. Luckily, I know how to get to Mark's pack from this highway.

'Wait,' I say. 'Is that a name or a commitment to service?'

Tristan chuckles a little. 'It's the doctor's real name,' he says. 'Rose's in good hands, don't worry. But she does need you here.'

'I'm getting there as fast as I can,' I say. The next exit is a smaller highway that heads off toward Mark's pack, so I take it. I'm going faster than this piece of shit van can probably handle, but I'll deal with that later.

'Kane?' I ask.

'Dead,' he says simply.

A combination of relief and anger wash over me. I wanted to kill the miserable asshole myself, but just knowing that Rose is no longer in danger from him is good enough for now.

'Well done,' I say. 'Any other threats looming?'

'None for now,' he tells me. 'We'll worry about that later. And I'll ask you all about what the hell took you so long later as well. But for now, how far out are you? These babies are just about ready to come out!'

'Twenty minutes, if this piece of shit I'm driving holds out,' I say. 'I'm on Highway 12.'

'I'll send warriors to meet you in something more reliable,' he says. 'Just keep driving.'

'You couldn't stop me if you tried,' I say.

'Ahhh!' screams Rose again. I'm not sure if she's screaming out loud as well as in the mind-link, but whatever helps her is great. It's also such an incredible relief to hear her voice again, even if she's cursing at me and screaming in pain. It's the pain of delivering my child, and that's the most beautiful thing in the world.

Tears start forming in my eyes, and Kelly comes up behind me and puts her arm around me.

"We'll be there soon," she says. "She'll be fine, and you'll be a father very soon."

"That makes me incredibly happy and incredibly nervous at the same time," I say. A million questions flow through my mind, all of them asking myself what kind of father I'll be. Will my child like me? Will they try to rebel because I wasn't a good enough father? Will he be a good citizen? Can I handle this responsibility for the rest of my life?

Kelly chuckles next to me. "I can see the wheels spinning in your head," she says. "You're going to be an incredible father, and Rose is going to be an unbelievably wonderful mother. All four of these babies have a great future ahead of them. And I can't wait to see them!"

"I'm sure you're right, but right now I can't even fathom the concept of fatherhood," I say.

"It'll be the most natural thing in the world to you once you lay your eyes on the baby," she says. "By the way, speaking of eyes, watch the road and focus. We have to get there in one piece first, new dad."

She giggles a little and returns to her seat next to Heather, who squeals in excitement when Kelly explains the situation to her.

The birth of my child is the most important thing that's ever happened in my life, and I need to be there for it. I hope and pray to the Moon Goddess that I'll get there in time.

'I'm almost there, baby,' I tell Rose as I press on the gas pedal.

CHAPTER 23: IT'S TIME

ROSE

We arrive at Mark's castle, finally, and as the Alphas are unloading me back out of the deathtrap of a van–not on a stretcher like any sensible people but by trying to carry my bloated body–I take a moment to look up at the beauty of the place.

I am in horrible pain, but the moment I look at the facade of the large building that resembles a large estate more than a castle, and a feeling of peace and tranquility suddenly settles around me.

It's beautiful. The Jacobethan architecture style, with its Renaissance flares and symmetrical wings in an off-white stone looks breathtaking with large red roses and other flowers blooming all along the front. The yard is a vivid green, and the sky behind the structure is bright blue. It is the picture of quaint country life on a grand scale, and I can imagine my children growing up here, running through the gardens, hiding amongst the willows, or feeding ducks in a large pond I am imagining sits in the back, though I can't see it.

Just as these pleasant thoughts bring a smile to my face, a horrendous pain shoots through me, and I am screaming bloody murder, lashing out, trying to hit anyone or anything nearby to make them understand how badly I need this pain to stop!

My fist catches Tristan in the eye, and then my other one hits Reece in the side of the head. They both stumble a bit, and then, I almost fall to the ground. "Why the fuck did you assholes not put me on a goddamn stretcher!" I shout at them.

"Sorry, baby," Reece says. "We should have. We are idiots."

"We're almost there," Mark insists, but it doesn't seem like we are getting any closer to the house to me.

"You had better not try to take my ass up any stairs when we get in there, or I swear to the Moon Goddess above, I will kill every last one of you! I will rip your hearts out with my own fingernails and shove them down your throats until you either suffocate or bleed to death!"

I see them exchanging glances, though Tristan has one eye shut either because his eye is swollen or because it just hurts, and I know they are worried. They are either worried that I really will kill them or worried that I have lost my very last marble.

Maybe they should be worried about both.

Getting me up the stairs to the porch is a tribulation as it is since there are so many of them, and I am so awkward. By the time they get me up, I am screaming in pain again, ready to just have this over with one way or another. If these babies don't hurry up and get out of me, I'm going to reach down there and pull them out myself!

A couple of servants are holding the doors open for us as the men get me through, and I am both relieved that it is a double door and mortified that I wouldn't fit through a single door. We enter a lovely foyer with marble on the floors and head to the left, and I am crying because I might not fit through the bedroom door.

But the room they take me to isn't a bedroom. It's some sort of a library or office. The bookshelves aren't very big, but the place is cozy, with a large fireplace flanked by one-footed wolves with snarling faces. It's not lit, thank the Goddess because I am burning up.

I am glad to see they have a bed set up for me here. They place me down on it, and I take a moment to try to get my emotions under control, but I am still crying at first and then screaming when the contractions strike again. I hate everything about this.

"If you don't give me a fucking epidural right this moment, I swear to the Goddess I will kill all of you!" I scream.

"Okay, okay. Let me check you, and we'll see what we can do." Dr. Travesty says as other people stream into the room who apparently have something to do with delivering babies. I look around and see four tiny little beds on wheels across the room from me, near what I assume is Mark's desk. The people are all ready for my babies, and I want to cry again.

The healers go about getting me dressed in a gown that's open in the back, like the hospital gowns, and I don't even care if there are forty-seven people in this room, I'm in so much pain, I'd lay here naked and have these babies. Then, she has me spread my legs with just a sheet over them and shoves her fingers all the way up to my throat.

It hurts like a son of a bitch!

"Yep, we've got time still," she says. Then, she turns to the people around her and starts giving orders for things I don't understand, but when she tells me to turn around and hang my feet off of the bed so she can look at my back, I almost freak out again.

"It's for the epidural," Mark says in a calm voice as he comes around to face me, taking my hands in his. "Let her put it in."

She has me curl my back, and then, I feel the prick of a needle and she says, "Okay, the epidural is in. It will take it a bit to get to work. Now, we'll start your IV and give you some other medicine to make you comfortable. Here's the button to push for when it hurts, but don't push it for–"

Before she can finish her sentence, I've already pushed the button about ten times.

Dr. Travesty swipes it from my hand. "Miss Rose! Are you trying to hurt yourself?"

"I'm already dying!" I say to her as another contraction hits me, and it isn't any easier than the ones before.

She shakes her head, and I want to punch her in the face, but I don't. She's got to have both eyes to get these babies out, unlike Tristan who is still winking at me.

They continue to bustle around me as I finally begin to settle into a state of minor pain and discomfort, and as the pain medication begins to work, I begin to feel much better about all of this. This is so easy, maybe I'll have four more babies.

About a half an hour goes by before Dr. Travesty checks me again. It's then that she says, "All right, Rose. It's time."

"Time for what?" I ask her, feeling a little loopy.

She has a silly smile on her face. "Why, time to push, of course," she says.

I look around. The Alphas are all smiling at me, too, and Tristan's eye looks better.

But something is wrong. Something isn't right. I can't push yet. I can't have these babies. "But... Eli's not here yet," I tell the doctor.

"I'm afraid these babies don't care," she says. "It's time to push."

"Don't worry. He's almost here," Reece says, squeezing my hand.

As Tristan lifts one leg and Mark lifts the other, I get ready to push–and I begin to cry.

'Eli? Where are you?'

CHAPTER 24: KILL THEM ALL

Kᴇʟʟʏ

"Thank the Goddess," I say. Cars are headed toward us on the horizon, and Eli has already received confirmation that they're Mark's warriors. They've come to meet us in some decent cars that won't fall apart on the highway like this piece of shit is threatening to do with every turn. At least now Eli can make it to Rose in time.

As they approach, I see that there are two cars, and one is a lot closer than the other. As it gets near, I can see why—it's a two-seater sports car, and it looks really fast.

Eli slows our van as we work out logistics. Obviously, the sports car is here for Eli so that he can get to Rose as fast as possible. I'd love to be there when the babies are born, but it's much more important that he get there on time. I probably wouldn't be in the birthing room with four Alphas taking up space anyway, so I'll wait until everything is done and the babies are brought out for me to see and hold.

I could just go with Eli and have one of us drive, but that car looks like a lot for me to handle and honestly, Eli shouldn't be driving anymore. The closer we've gotten to Rose, the more nervous he's become. I guess that's typical of an expectant father, and I think it's kind of cute, but he really needs to get there in one piece. Whoever's driving the car right now looks like he knows what he's doing, so I'll just let him get Eli to the maternity ward on time.

After a bit of discussion, Eli brings the van to a stop and jumps out just as the sports car reaches us. He doesn't waste any time hopping in, then the driver speeds off. I guess the babies are arriving sooner than we thought. I hope he makes it on time.

That leaves me with Heather, Eustace, Brent, and Sean. There's only one other car, and it's still headed down the highway.

"I'd better drive 'er in," says Eustace, nodding his head toward the driver's seat of our old van. I doubt the thing will make it back to their pack without falling apart or running out of gas, so I suppose we'd better let him follow us back to Mark's pack to regroup and maybe get the poor thing fixed properly.

As the car pulls up beside us, we see that there are only three seats.

"Heather, you come with me," I say. "Brent and Sean, do you want to go with Eustace or ride shotgun with us?"

"I'd better go with Eustace," says Brent. "I don't want him getting lost or stranded out here."

"Me, too," says Sean, "unless you'd feel more comfortable if I ride with you."

I shake my head. Eli has already verified that these are Mark's people, so I trust them completely. "You guys go ahead," I say.

"I'm kind of attached to this old van," says Sean. "I'd love to see her make it on her own."

Guys are strange. I laugh and shake my head to express that thought, then climb into the back seat of the car as the boys take off in that raggedy van. It's going surprisingly fast; I guess they're trying to compete with the sports car. Men, good grief.

I'm fastening my seatbelt and look up to see that Heather is still outside, wide-eyed.

"Heather?" I ask. "What's wrong?"

"I just... I just ain't never seen nothin' as nice as this before," she says. Apparently, she's impressed with the car. It is a pretty nice luxury sedan, and the seats are the most comfortable thing I've been in for a long time, so I'm a little impressed as well, I suppose.

I laugh. "Heather, you lived in a luxury resort," I say. "There were plenty of nice things there." It was true, although most of those nice things were pretty old and run-down. But they were still nice. "Hop in."

She finally snaps out of it and steps inside.

"I'm Chris," says the driver. "What say we get you ladies to your destination?"

I nod. "We're ready!"

The ride is smooth as we head down the highway, and I look out the window, enjoying the view. The sun is setting out on the horizon, and the rolling hills are taking on a pinkish hue, with golden rays of the last hint of sunlight filtering through soft, fluffy clouds. It's a beautiful scene, and it's ideal to set the mood for what's ahead. Rose is safe, the babies are being born, and I'm confident that Eli will get there in time to witness the first seconds of his journey into fatherhood. Everything is perfect.

But then my head juts sideways suddenly, crashing into the window at the same time that Chris yells, "Oh, shit!" from the driver's seat.

I hear Heather scream, followed by the sound of breaking glass and crunching metal as the entire car flips over. I try to reach over to hold her, but I can't even control my own body as the car continues to flip.

We finally come to a stop, and I strain to move my head to see if Heather is okay. She's moving and moaning, but Chris looks bloody, hanging halfway out of the front windshield. And he's not moving at all.

I try to get my bearings. Somehow the car has landed upright after who knows how many flips, but the space inside is noticeably smaller from the twisted metal. I undo my seatbelt and try to scoot over closer to Heather to check her out better, unfastening her seatbelt as well so we can get out of the car, if it's even possible to open the doors.

My head is pounding, and I'm just reaching for the door latch when I see movement outside. The door opens before I can get it done myself. At first, I'm relieved. Someone must have seen the accident and stopped on the highway to help us.

But that quickly fades away as I hear Heather scream. I look over to see her being pulled roughly out the door on the other side, then I suddenly feel someone yanking on my arm while some sort of cloth is yanked over my head.

I start to shift but don't get the chance to get into my wolf form as I feel a prick in the side of my neck, and the world quickly goes black.

ADAM

"You called for me, Your Majesty?" I ask. It's an understatement because he's been screaming at me for the last fifteen minutes, which is how long it takes to jog from my room to his quarters. Well, he was actually mind-link screaming, but that can be even worse because it always gives me a sharp, pounding headache.

"Adam!" he bellows as I jog up to him in the hallway. "It's about fucking time, you incompetent idiot! You're fired!"

"I... what, Your Majesty?"

"I said, you're fucking fired! I have a new Beta, one who's going to get the fucking job done right!"

"Job...." I say, and then I catch sight of the man standing beside King Gene.

I've seen him around the castle, but I hadn't looked twice at the man before. Now that he's standing right in front of me, I examine his demeanor. Something isn't quite right, and I can't put a finger on it at first. He looks normal enough, even friendly in a way, completely relaxed and confident as he stands to his full height next to the king, making Gene look like some sort of child's toy in comparison.

But when I look into his icy blue eyes, I see it—a cold, calculating intent that sends a chill down my spine.

"Yes, you fucking idiot," says Gene, and I just notice that he's still talking. "I hereby officially fire you as my Beta and appoint Alastor Dravenwolf as Beta of Black Rock to assist me as I rule the kingdom!"

I'm in complete shock and just stand here, staring at these men. Gene walks away, and I can see a light smirk pass over Alastor's face as he turns and follows behind him. I'm left standing there in the hall-way, realizing that my mouth is still open. I close it and follow quietly, standing next to the door they've just entered, the king's private suite.

"Fucking moron," Gene says. "Glad to be rid of him. Now, you're clear on your first assignment, are you not? These Alphas and their spawn are a threat to my crown, and the longer they breathe the same air as me, they'll interfere in my role as the rightful rule."

"Yes, Your Majesty," says Alastor.

Hearing his haunting voice for the first time restores the chills throughout my body I felt earlier .

"Good then," says Gene. "The four Alphas, the breeder, and all of those miserable Alpha-spawned brats that are crawling out of her— kill them all."

CHAPTER 25: FOUR BABIES FOR FOUR ALPHAS

ROSE

"What do you mean you need me to push, you ugly bitch?" Even though I have the epidural, it's not completely made the pain go away, and whenever I have a contraction, I'm beginning to feel it again. I asked Dr. Travesty if I could have a new button because the one I've been pushing recently doesn't seem to be working to send more meds, and she said no.

Can you fucking believe it?

She said it wasn't the button, it was the epidural itself, that I'd used it all up already, and while she would put a new one in if I needed it, she didn't think I did. She said I'd be able to push better if I could feel it a little.

What the actual fuck? I don't want to feel it a little. I don't want to feel it at all! I want the goddessdamn medicine!

But I don't have any choice. She says in a soothing voice that irritates the fuck out of me, "Now, now, Miss Rose, it will be all right. One of your babies is right here, ready to come out. So just give the children a little push, and soon enough, this will all be over, and you'll have your babes in your arms, and you'll forget all about it."

I think her words are meant to be inspiring and calming, but they really make me want to scream and run away from this place. One of my babies has its giant head pressed to the entrance of my va-jay-jay, and it's ready to tear my tiny hole to shreds because that's the only way it knows how to get out? What's more, that one has three others behind it?

"Isn't there another way?" I ask, tears beginning to stream down my face.

"No, not for you," Dr. Travesty says in that same mellow voice. "Your babies are all perfectly lined up, not causing any commotion, and can easily slide right out through the birth canal. We only go the other way when we have to. Recovering from surgery isn't the way to start off raising four small children."

"Cut me open!" I scream as Tristan squeezes my leg. "I don't wanna push them out!"

"Rose, darling," Mark says, leaning over and brushing the tears off of my cheeks. "It'll be all right. You can do this."

"Maybe I can," I say, not doubting my abilities to push them out. I'm strong, and even with the epidural and a lack of complete feeling, I think I can do it. I'm just scared to. "But what if... what if... it ruins me?"

The men exchange a confused glance that almost has me wanting to smack each of them again. "Ruins you?" Reece asks, brushing my hair over my shoulders. Of all the times to forget a ponytail holder....

"That's right," I say, fighting more tears. "What if it leaves a giant, gaping hole in my who-ha, and you guys can't even feel me anymore? You'll get tired of me, you'll find someone else, and you'll all leave me! Isn't it enough that my body has had to stretch to the size of Mt. Vesuvius to accommodate all of these fucking babies? Now I've got to create a cavern between my legs so that they can make their grand entrance to the world!"

Again, they are all looking at one another before they begin to chuckle. Now, I want to kill them all. "Get out!" I scream and point to the door. "And I'm not talking to the babies! I mean their fathers!"

Tristan jumps in. "Rose, baby, little flower, you don't have to worry about that. You will always feel amazing to us, even if your body doesn't quite go back to how it was before. And you will always look beautiful to us, even if you are a little bigger than you were before you had our children. We love you for you, not for what you look like. And we love making love to you because of how it is to be with you."

"Don't worry about that, baby," Mark says as Reece nods in agreement.

"I'd hate to interrupt," Dr. Travesty says in a sing-song voice, "but this one with the dark hair is ready to come out now!"

With new determination, I bear down and begin to push. I grit my teeth as Reece counts for me, and with Dr. Travesty's help, I only have to push a few times before she tells me to stop.

And then... I see her.

Tiny, purple and red with white goo all over her, and mad as hell, she's holding a baby girl, my baby girl, with curly black hair and the fiercest little fists flying.

"Oh, my Goddess!" I say as I cover my mouth with both hands. She is the most beautiful thing I've ever seen in my life.

"Is that mine?" Tristan asks, and he has tears streaming down his face. "Is that my daughter?"

"We won't know until we do some tests, but... it appears to. She definitely has your hair," Dr. Travesty says.

They lift the baby onto my stomach, and Tristan cuts the umbilical cord. The moment she rests on me, she stops crying, and I kiss her little head. Her face is scrunched up, and I can tell that she is still shaken, but she feels safe so close to my heartbeat.

I can't hold her for long, though, as another baby is coming. A nurse sweeps my daughter away, going to clean her up, she says, and then I have to bear down and push.

The next screams are of a little girl with dark hair, but it's not unruly, and she has Reece's nose to be sure, so we assume this girl is his, and he cuts the cord.

In my head, I hear Eli's voice. 'I'm almost there, my love!'

'Hurry!' I tell him. 'I haven't seen a redheaded baby yet, but... I can't wait much longer!'

After they take my second daughter to be cleaned and swaddled, I push again, and a little light-haired boy with a very serious demeanor comes out. He is the fastest to come out as well, once I started pushing, and I have no doubt that he's Mark's son as I stare down at his face. He is looking back at me in wonder as I stroke his cheek.

"All right. One more time," the doctor says. "And we need to hurry."

They take Mark's son from me, and I notice something I haven't before about the way Dr. Travesty is acting. She seems less light-hearted now, which is odd because she is always so bouncy and kind, despite her name.

But I'm not ready yet. "Eli is almost here," I tell her. "I believe it's his baby next."

"We cannot wait." Dr. Travesty's tone send a shiver down my spine. She turns to a nurse and tells her something, and she nods and rushes out of the room.

"Doc, is everything all right?" I can tell by Mark's tone he is concerned as well.

Dr. Travesty clears her throat. "I'm not certain right now, but I do know we need to get this baby out quickly. Rose, push."

Her order sounds like it came from the mouth of an Alpha, so I don't argue. I bear down and push, wishing Eli were here.

After three pushes, I am exhausted, and the room is spinning. I feel faint. I want to lay down, but Dr. Travesty is yelling at me. "Rose, you must push again, and you must do it now!" she orders.

It seems like she's standing further away from me now, and little particles of light are dancing all around her. It's an odd sensation, like she's at the end of a kaleidoscope.

"Rose?" Tristan sounds worried. I try to focus my eyes on him, but I can't.

"What's happening?" I mutter.

"Rose! Push!" Dr. Travesty commands, so I do.

I hear a noise at the door, but I am distracted by pushing with everything I have left in me. As I hear the baby begin to cry, I see a mop of red hair on his head, and my eyes connect for a second with a man whose head is adorned with the same lustrous locks.

"You're here. Eli…." My voice is a whisper, and even before they put my son on my chest, I fall back onto the pillows. My eyes won't stay open….

Everything fades away.

CHAPTER 26: BECOMING A FATHER

Eli

Now, this is a vehicle. I'm so thankful that I was finally able to reach Rose, and that the other Alphas rushed these cars out to meet us. That old piece of shit van held out for a lot longer than I'd expected, but this... this thing is fast, and I know it'll get me to Rose fast.

I'm going to have to get myself one of these.

I guess that won't work, though, because I'm about to become a father, and there's definitely no room for a baby's car seat in here. Maybe I'll get one for Rose and me to take quiet rides in the country-side together once the baby is grown.

I guess I can't really think about kids growing up and moving out yet when this is the very day that I become a father for the first time. There's just so much going through my head that I can't even keep a coherent thought in there for longer than a few seconds.

A son? A daughter? Will I be training up another Alpha, teaching him how to be a strong, fair leader and how to treat his mate with respect and love? Or will I be watching a mini version of my beautiful Rose grow into a delightful young woman, destined to be a future Luna? If she's even half as gorgeous as Rose, which I'm sure she will be, I'll have to fight off the boys all the way from puberty through her twenty-first birthday.

I can see it now—some smartass young Alpha's son thinking he has any business even attempting to date my daughter. And if he dares to treat her like anything else than a goddess and a princess… I'll kill him.

Okay, I'm getting away from myself. Maybe it'll be a son, and I won't have to worry about any of that. Either way, the child I have with Rose is going to be loved and cherished through his or her life. I smile as I look out the window, watching the stunning pink and golden sunset that's signaling the birth of my child.

I just hope that Rose's all right.

'Hurry up!' she keeps hollering in my head, sometimes accompanied by some not-so-sweet words, but any words my beautiful Rose— my mate—is babbling in the throes of labor as she has my child are a pure treasure. 'You fucking idiot! Get your ass here right now before I punch you!' Ahh… the sweet music of true love.

I look over at the driver, realizing that I haven't said a word to the man since he picked me up. He's pretty intent on driving right now, and that's great, but I guess I should be polite since he's getting me to Rose quickly.

"Thank you," I say. "I'm guessing you know this, but I'm Alpha Eli. What's your name?"

"Chuck," he says, taking his eyes off the road for only a split second to shoot a smile in my direction. "And you have the look of a man about to be a father for the first time. I've been there, and believe me, your life is about to change forever. It's in a good way, of course. And you'll do fine."

"I hope you're right," I say. "I just want to be the best father I can possibly be."

"We all do," he says. "And right now, you can't possibly imagine what it's going to really be like when you first look your little pup in the eye, but once you do, fatherhood will become second nature."

"You make it sound so easy," I say, chuckling a little.

"It is," he says. "And it's not. But every day you'll be stronger in a way you never imagined. As young shifters, we spend all this time strengthening our muscles, our fighting skills. And in school, we sharpen our brains. That's all good and well, especially for an Alpha like you who will rule the pack. But our children strengthen something you never knew you had inside of you. I can't even put a name on it. Resolve, maybe? Tenacity?" He shook his head. "Nope, none of those words even come close. But you'll feel it, and you'll know it's there, and you'll know it makes you stronger."

"You sound experienced in all this," I say.

He laughs. "Three daughters and one set of twins—sons," he says. "Now believe me, that's experience."

"No doubt," I say. I notice the twinkling in his eyes as he mentions his children. Will I have the same look about me when I'm finally a father?

He focuses back on the road and steps on the gas a little harder, so I let him concentrate on driving while I watch the scenery fly by—and it really is flying. I wasn't that far from Mark's castle to begin with, so I'm sure we're almost there.

Sure enough, I see a huge estate appearing on the horizon a few moments later. Even from far away I can see that it's majestic, surrounded by lush greenery—exactly how I pictured Mark's domain.

We get closer, and I see that everything is well cared-for, as is always the case when a great leader is in charge. As we approach, I notice some well-manicured flower gardens and wide-open green spaces, but I can't really concentrate on any of that because the closer we get, the more knots form in my stomach.

It's not a sense of dread, not at all. It's excitement mixed with fear mixed with uncertainty. I've been to more battles than I can count, but the jittery feeling I experience before those has nothing on the inten sity of this experience.

I barely let Chuck come to a stop in front of the castle before I open the door and jump out. I don't even manage to say goodbye to Chuck, or to thank him, and I make a note somewhere in the back of my head to do so later, but with five pups of his own, I know he understands how I feel right now.

He's thankfully mind-linked about my arrival ahead it seems, because servants come pouring out of the front entrance and run right up to me.

"Alpha Eli," says an older woman who looks like the kind of person you wouldn't ever ignore when she's talking to you. "Come with me."

I nod and she leads me—thankfully quickly since she's spryer than she appears outwardly—down a maze of hallways that I would never be able to navigate on my own.

"How much farther?" I ask. "How is Rose?"

"She's fine, Alpha Eli," she says. "And you'll be able to ask her your-self very shortly. But first—" She ushers me into a room with a sink and towels. "You need to wash up, sir. I don't mean to offend, but you do look like you've been knee-deep in... oil? And we can't have you holding a newborn pup with those arms."

I'd forgotten what a mess I am from working on the van, and she's right. I let her lead me to the sink, where she provided a huge bottle of liquid soap that smelled like oranges, a scrubbing brush, and then eventually a towel. I washed up quicker and more thoroughly than I ever had in my life, and when she did a quick inspection, I felt like a five-year-old again having to make sure that my mother approved of my cleanliness before a formal dinner.

But I'm no five-year-old. I'm an Alpha who is about to become a father. The woman—I don't have time to ask her name—half-grabs me by the sleeve and ushers me back the way we came.

And then... I feel her and experience the fragrance of her beautiful scent before I hear her crying out. It's my Rose, and she's part shout-ing, part cursing, and part apologizing. Mostly shouting and cursing.

The woman leading me slams the door open, and I run in just in time to see Rose push, and like magic, a beautiful pup with bright red locks comes out, and my world changes in an instant, just like Chuck had said.

"You're here, Eli..."

I hear Rose's voice, and I want to run to my mate, but I'm so captivated by this beautiful child—he's a boy, they tell me—that I can't take my eyes off him. They even let me cut the umbilical cord.

The nurse cleans him up quickly and hands him to me, his beautiful blue eyes blinking at the bright lights. He's the tiniest thing I've ever seen in my life, but he may as well be as huge as the biggest mountain by the way he's captured my attention… and my instant love.

I sense the other Alphas around me as well as the medical personnel in the room, but for a few beautiful moments, it's like the world is nothing but me and my son.

But then I notice a mood change, and the air in the room is suddenly heavy with a chill that makes me want to take my son, run away, and hide with him forever. It's the deepest sense of fear and foreboding that I've ever felt, and it hangs over the room like a fog.

Finally, I break eye contact with my son and look up, noticing the influx of more medical personnel rushing into the room. I look at the other Alphas and they're all staring at the bed, so I follow their gaze and my eyes see Rose.

But she's not looking back…. She doesn't seem to be responding to the world around her at all.

And a huge puddle of deep, dark blood is pooling on the floor.

CHAPTER 27:SHE CAN'T BE DEAD

Mark

My mouth is dry and my cheeks are wet as I stare at Rose's beautiful face. The healers and nurses are running around, doing everything they can, and all I can do is stand here, feeling helpless.

It's not like me at all. I'm used to taking charge, figuring things out, saving the day.

But it's Dr. Travesty who is making commands, ordering people around as she stands at the foot of the bed, blood up to her elbows, doing everything she can to save our precious Rose–my beautiful, intelligent, lovely Rose.

The other Alphas are just as stunned as I am. Tristan has his mouth hanging open, and Reece's face is streaked with tears. Eli has just gotten here when the crisis began, so it took him a moment to realize what was going on.

Now, as a nurse insists he hand over his son so the baby can be cleaned up, he does so and takes a few steps closer to where the other three of us are gathered around her bed.

"Start a transfusion!" Dr. Travesty is shouting. "I need a better clamp!"

I don't know what she's talking about, and I don't want to interrupt her to see if there's anything I can do. I know nothing about birthing babies or saving lives, but it seems to me that the enormous dark pool of blood on the floor isn't a sign that all is well.

Nor is the fact that Rose's eyes are closed, and her face is growing paler by the instant.

Eli is standing next to Tristan now, and I see the confusion on his face. "What's happening?" It's just a whisper, but none of us dare to try and articulate the response. Saying it out loud might make it so.

How do I even formulate those words on my tongue? To tell him what's going on with our sweet Rose? A thousand thoughts rush through my head, and I am taken back to the beginning. That day, in the hallway, in Dark Forest Castle, when Tristan and I were on our way to speak to the king.

We'd decided this entire endeavor was ridiculous. It was idiotic to choose a new ruler this way, and none of the four of us were happy about the prospect of sharing a woman. We'd spoken to Reece and Eli, and we'd come up with another plan. We'd simply have a series of contests to decide who would be the next in line for the throne. We'd each go about finding our fated mates, and whoever the king was, they would have a child with their mate to take the throne after them. It was simple enough.

But then we'd seen her....

Rose had crashed right into us on her way to the clinic, and she'd taken our breath away. Both of us had immediately felt drawn to her. After she scurried away, we'd agreed–if that's the winner, we'll find a way to make this work.

Miraculously, a short time later, we were introduced to Rose as the winner. Our breeder. And the four of us knew this was meant to be.

The four Alphas would gladly share Rose just to have a chance to be with her.

it was both the most absurd and most meaningful thing I'd ever done in my life.

I think back to our first night alone together, how fortunate I'd felt to have won that race and to get to claim her. But it was also a great deal of responsibility. She was a delicate, precious flower, and I'd been so frightened to hurt her.

It had been one of the best nights of my life.

All of the nights with Rose were like that. Every time she was in my arms, her head on my chest, her heart beating against mine… it was like a new piece of heaven was gifted to me every time.

It wasn't just the sex, though. I thought of her laughing, smiling face out in the sunshine on our picnic, how beautiful she was when she sang, how she looked so serious when she was reading her book and was interrupted.

I thought about all of the hard times she'd gone through just to get here. How her parents had been so cruel to her, I will never understand. She made it through the trials of growing up in that awful place, though. Then, at the castle, there had been numerous attempts on her life. She'd had to put up with Emily and then Barbara. King Gene had a plan to kill her.… Nothing ever came easy for Rose.

She never truly complained, though. Sure, she'd joke about how the pups had her so big and uncomfortable, taking jabs at herself for being so round and heavy, but that was only because her body was doing something extraordinary, something no one else could do. She was carrying our four babies, all at the same time. That made her even more special than she had been before.

And I love her for it, Goddess do I love her. Looking at her face now, seeing her so still and unmoving, I can't help the sobs that start to emit from my throat. I don't give a fuck that everyone in this room can see me crying like a child. I drop to my knees next to her bed, out of Dr. Travesty's way, holding Rose's hand in my hand, noting that it's colder than it should be. "Please, Rose, please don't leave us. We need you so bad!" I choke out between sobs.

I don't have to look at the other Alphas to know they are crying just as hard as I am. All of us are begging her now, praying to the Moon Goddess to spare her. She carried our pups, and now, she won't even get to hold them? To see them grow up? No, it can't end that way! We fought so hard for this day, for her to be able to stay in our lives, in our children's lives. We refuse to let her slip away.

A whirlwind of activity goes on around us, and a healer steps over me to put something in Rose's arm. I glance over to see a bag of blood, and immediately, I stand, wiping at my eyes. "I'm type O," I say, rolling up my sleeve.

"Good because that's our last bag of A positive," Dr. Travesty says. "Listen, gentlemen, I know it looks bleak. I was able to repair the damage inside of Miss Rose's body, but she has lost an insane amount of blood. If we can get her more quickly enough, she does stand a chance."

"She's not dead?" Reece clarifies.

Dr. Travesty shakes her head. "No. Her heart is still beating, though it's faint. Mark, if you can give us another pint or two...."

"I'll give you every last drop," I say as a healer approaches with the appropriate medical tools to harvest my life force.

Dr. Travesty gives me a sympathetic smile as I'm guided into a chair. "That won't be necessary. I can't take one life to save another. But I will take as much as you can safely give."

"I'm A positive," Tristan announces, and soon he is hooked up with a needle in his arm.

Eli and Reece continue to stay right next to Rose, brushing back her hair and praying over her.

Dr. Travesty looks exhausted as she instructs the maids to clean the floor. It's stone, so it won't need to be replaced, but that's the least of my worries.

"One more thing, gentlemen," the doctor says. "I hope that four babies are enough for you because... unfortunately, I wasn't able to save Rose's reproductive organs."

"Her two uterine horns?" Eli asks.

The doctor nods. "All of it had to come out to save her life."

"That's okay," I say for all of us. "We have four beautiful, healthy babies."

"That's right," the doctor says. "All of the babies are doing well. So... as soon as their mother is ready, she'll be able to hold them."

I'm beginning to feel a bit lightheaded from the blood leaving my body, but I look over at Rose, and I see her face is a shade more pink, and I begin to think perhaps she has a chance.

CHAPTER 28: TRAPPED

KELLY

My eyes open, but I still can't see anything, though my eyesight is very sharp even when I'm not in wolf form. I've got a strange feeling washing over me; everything feels muffled and confused, and I can't even think straight.

Then I remember it—the crash, the flipping car, Heather's screaming, the people dragging us out. "Heather!" I scream.

"I… I'm here," she says from somewhere. I'm not sure if she's even in the same room or not, because it sounds far away, hollow, like she's talking through some sort of iron pipe or something.

I try to shift and somehow, I'm completely blocked from doing it no matter how hard my mind tries to focus. The next step is a mind-link to call Eli, but that's also oddly blank, so I start to feel panic rising up in my chest. Is there a powerful Alpha around here who can block my shifting and mind-link? Kane is dead, so it's not him. But I don't think Alpha Stephen or anyone else is powerful enough to block my mind-link. At least, I don't think so. I've never experienced it before.

"Are you okay?" I ask Heather.

She doesn't answer for a moment, so I'm worried, but then she chimes in with a weak voice, "I think so. I... I don't know. Where are we?"

I shake my head but know she can't see me in this pitch darkness. "I don't know," I say. "But I'm going to find out." I try to stand up but instantly get yanked back down by something holding my hands together. It's metal, handcuffs probably, and they're very tight. My head had been too foggy to notice them before. I take a deep breath and try to adjust my eyes. There has to be some sliver of light in here somewhere.

"Kelly?" says Heather. "I can't... move. I'm scared."

"It's okay," I say, although I'm not convinced that it's okay at all. "I'm going to reach Alpha Eli, and he's going to find us. We'll be okay."

"But I... I can't even talk 'ta Eustace," she says. "Why can't I?"

"I'm not sure," I say. I debate for a moment whether I should tell her I can't reach Eli, either. She may have had a hard life, but she's still young, almost still a child, really. In fact, maybe she's even more of a child because she's led that hard life. I don't want to panic her, so I decide to keep that quiet.

All I can do now is try to assess my situation. The darkness tells me that we must be underground. If we're just in an interior room, we'd see some sort of light through the cracks, I would think. I'm sitting on a floor, and it's cold, and clearly, I'm attached to something low with these handcuffs because I can't stand up.

The fogginess in my head is only clearing up a little bit. Did they drug me? I can't remember.

A huge clanking sound startles me so much that I jump and instantly try to shift, but it's still not working. Blinding light shoots into the room and I have to close my eyes because it's so bright, it physically hurts. Then I hear loud footsteps.

"Kelly?" whispers Heather.

I try to reach for her, but I can't move, and she's too far away.

ADAM

"What!?" Shelby is screaming at me, and I'm pacing around the room. I've just told her of my demotion, and clearly, she isn't taking it well.

"I wish that was the worst part of all this," I say.

"There's more?!"

She's getting louder, so I gesture with my hands that we need to keep it down. I don't really want her screaming in my head and giving me a headache, but I have no choice but to take this conversation to another level.

'He's got some new crony, and he wants him to kill everyone,' I say in the mind-link.

'Kill everyone?!' She's still yelling, and yes, it's already giving me a headache. 'Kill who?'

'Everyone,' I say. 'The Alphas, Rose... even the pups. He wants them all killed.'

'But... but why? What did those four innocent pups do to him?' she says. 'Adam, you have to stop him.'

'I know,' I say. I wish it were that easy. 'I know. But I don't know how. I need help figuring this out.'

'Well, who is this crony guy?' she asks. 'Do you really think he'll kill innocent babies?'

'He sure seems the type,' I say. 'His name is Alastor Dravenwolf. Heard of him?'

'The name sounds familiar, but can't say I remember exactly,' she says. "What are we going to do?" She asks the last question out loud, but in a whisper.

"I need to warn the Alphas, but no one has answered me lately," I say.

She nods. "Well, they're new fathers," she says. "Come to think of it, no one's messaged me, either. I know Rose would want to tell me right away about the babies and would have them message us. You don't think something's gone wrong?"

"Goddess, I hope not," I say.

"No," she says, shaking her head. "I'm sure things are fine. Giving birth to four pups is quite a feat, so I'm sure she's exhausted. She's probably just gazing into each of their little eyes right now and has completely forgotten that the rest of the world even exists."

"Probably," I say. Now I'm worried. That threat from Gene sure sounded like he meant business, and I know nothing about Alastor. If they're not answering, maybe he's gotten his hands on them all already…

"Actually," she says. "Something is wrong."

"Why?" I ask.

"Kelly," she says. "The moment those pups came out, she would have told me. She's with Eli. So either Eli hasn't reached Mark's castle yet, or something really is wrong. Oh, Adam. What can we do?!"

"We'll get some intel from this end," I say. "He may have fired me, but Gene is too far gone to pay any attention to me listening in on him."

"Well, I'm going with you," she says, reaching for her shoes.

"I don't want you involved in this," I say. "I think it's better if you just stay here. If they think I'm up to something, you could be in danger. I have no idea what this Alastor person is even capable of."

"Oh, no," she says. "You don't get to play the 'protect the women-folk' card with me. I'm going with you. Anything you're in for, I'm in for right with you. Do you really think I'd be safe if they thought you were a spy anyway? They'd haul me down to that miserable dungeon to sit in Barbara's old cage, or worse."

Ugh, Barbara—I'd forgotten about her. Gene is pretty harmless, but if that Alastor guy and Barbara team up, we could all be in serious trouble. "Don't remind me of that useless bitch," I say. "We have to keep an eye on her, too. I think that's the best thing we can do for the Alphas and Rose right now."

"Okay, makes sense," she says. "So that's two people who need watching, and we're two people, so that's perfect. I can manage to be wherever Barbara is, but I think I'd stick out like a sore thumb if I hang out around Gene's room. He might think I'm trying to… Oh, Goddess, I'm not even going to go there. I'll just watch Barbara. Where is she?"

I have no idea where Barbara is, and she's the one I'm supposed to be watching, according to the Alphas. If they knew about Alastor, I'm sure they'd want us to keep an eye on both of them.

"I really don't know," I say, and I get 'the glare,' which means it's time for me to get out of here. Shelby can be scary when she wants to be. She's gorgeous and sexy, but frightening whenever she thinks I'm doing something stupid.

"I'll find her," she says after a brief stare-off.

"Alright," I say. "Be careful. Keep trying to reach the Alphas. Whichever of us reaches them first, ask the Alphas to bring the other into the mind-link and we'll figure this out."

"Alright," she says, pulling me into her arms and kissing me passionately. We linger for a moment, letting each other bask in the delicious taste of our mate, then we part, both heading down opposite ends of the hallway.

'Don't do anything stupid,' she says in my mind.

CHAPTER 29: THIS IS WHAT IT'S LIKE TO BE DEAD

Rose

I hear voices in the distance. It's foggy–like they are in another room, through a closed door, maybe underwater. I can't really understand what they're saying, but I recognize some of them.

My brain feels heavy, like a sponge that's soaked up too much water and is dripping onto the floor. Why can't I think clearly? I can't even remember what I was doing.

It seems a bit ironic to me that I was pretending not to remember anything when I woke up in Alpha Kane's castle, and now, as I attempt to blink my eyes, I really can't remember much of anything.

Thinking of Alpha Kane has my heart racing for a moment. Is he still nearby? Are my babies in danger? I want to lift my hand to protect my abdomen, as I often do, but my arms feel like they weigh a thousand pounds each, and I really can't move at all.

What's going on? Is it the drugs he gave me? It seems like I've already dealt with all of that….

And then, I remember.

I remember the pain, the uncomfortableness, the stairs, the van, arriving at Mark's castle, the medicine… and the babies!

I had my babies! I gave birth to all four of them. I'd seen their little faces with my own eyes!

So... why couldn't I wake up to hold them now?

"She looks so peaceful," I hear Tristan say. I know it's him. I recognize his voice, and he's close by. I can understand him.

'Like she's just asleep," Reece replies.

"The most beautiful woman in the world," Mark adds.

"I was hoping to have a chance to kiss her again," Eli laments.

Eli?

Eli!

Eli is here! I'd seen him, too.

I needed to open my eyes so I could be with my men and my babies. But I wasn't able to.

Their words went back through my mind, and as the meaning behind them began to sink in, I realized what they were talking about.

It all became very clear to me now. I can't open my eyes. I can't move. I can't speak–because I'm dead!

How had this happened? Why would the Moon Goddess let this happen to me? I'd come so far! I'd carried my babies to full-term and given birth to them! I'd fought so hard to keep them safe against the likes of Emily, Barbara, King Gene, Alpha Robert, Alpha Winston, and that awful Alpha Kane. Now, after all of that, I hadn't even gotten to tell them I love them!

Tears form in my eyes. At least, it seems that tears are forming in my eyes. I'm not sure if that's possible or if it's just my imagination, what with me being dead and all. The more I think about my wonderful Alphas, my precious babies, and all of the friends I've made that I'm leaving behind, the more I cry.

"Are those... tears?" I think I hear Tristan ask.

"Is she crying?" That's Reece.

"I think she might be!" Mark chimes in.

"Rose? Rose, baby, can you hear us?" Eli asks me.

I still can't answer them, but the fact that they can see that I am upset makes me think perhaps I'm not dead after all. I use all of the energy I have left inside of me to try and open my eyes. I just need to see their faces again.

With all of my concentration on just my right eye, after several seconds, I'm finally able to lift my eyelid just a bit. It falls closed again, but I'm not willing to give up. I blink a couple of times, and then both of my eyes are working, and I'm awake–I'm alive!

"Rose!" all four of them sing out, laughing and smiling. It's hard to focus, but I look from one face to another, and my heart is full with happiness as I realize I am still alive and the blessings that the Moon Goddess has poured out upon me are all right here.

The four Alphas are standing next to my bed, and in their arms, each of them is holding a beautiful baby–my babies.

Eli brushes the tears off my cheeks. "Goddess, I'm so happy to see you. How are you, beautiful?"

My mouth is dry, and it takes a lot of strength to croak out. "Alive." They all laugh, but I didn't mean it as a joke.

"Of course you are," Tristan tells me, standing right next to my left shoulder. "We would never let anything happen to you, little flower."

A moment later, I hear another familiar voice and cringe. "Move aside, gentlemen!" It's Dr. Travesty. I was sort of hoping I'd never see her again. Clearly, her name is bad luck.

But then, she did deliver my babies, and I am alive, so there's that.

"Oh, Miss Rose!" she says. "You gave us quite a scare. I'm so glad you're back around now. Let me do a quick check."

"Wh-what happened?" I ask as she begins to listen to my heart and lungs.

"You lost a lot of blood during the deliveries," Mark explains to me, and I can hear traces of sadness and fear in his voice. "We were afraid it was too much."

"But the doc gave you some transfusions and patched everything up," Reece tells me.

I can't imagine how scary that must've been for all of them. All I can think to say is, "I'm sorry."

"Don't be sorry." Eli says. 'We're just so thankful you're all right now."

"She is all right, isn't she?" Tristan asks the doctor.

Dr. Travesty nods her head. "She is. Miss Rose, you will need some time to rest and recover, but I see no reason why you won't be just fine in a few days' time."

That makes my heart sing. "Thank you, Doctor," I tell her, so glad that she was here after all, since she apparently saved my life.

"Now, why don't we let this mama hold her babies?" she says, stepping aside.

The men help me sit up, and then, one by one, they place their children on my lap. I look them over through my tears, unable to believe how beautiful they are. Two little girls, and two little boys. I can see their fathers' faces in each of theirs, but I can also see myself, and they are worth every moment of agony I've gone through since I got on that train.

I'm crying again, but it's with an overwhelming sense of happiness. I can't imagine anything in the world ever being wrong again as long as I have these beautiful babies and these four amazing men.

As awful as it was, I can't help but declare, "I think... one day... I might want to do this again!"

The men exchange wide-eyed glances, and I think they might just be scared of the prospect of us having eight children.

But then, Mark murmurs, "Do you want me to tell her?"

"Tell me what?" I ask, fear building up inside of my chest.

No one is saying anything in response, and as I continue to shift my eyes from one of them to the next, I become more and more frightened. "Tell me what?"

Mark clears his throat and says, "Dr. Travesty had to... take out... your... reproductive organs."

"What?" I can't believe what he's telling me. "What does that mean?"

"It means we won't be able to have any more children," Reece explains. "But that's okay. Because we have these four, and we have each other."

"And we'll still be able to have sex," Tristan chimes in. I turn and look at him, narrowing my eyes. He shrugs. "I just wanted to make sure that part was clear."

Eli says, "We're so sorry, Rose. But it was the only way to save you."

Disappointment rolls over me, but I understand.

I look down at my little bundles and know that they're the only children I will ever have, so I will be the best mom I can possibly be.

Even if it kills me.

After all, I've already been dead once.

And I lived to tell about it.

CHAPTER 30: A BEAUTIFUL EXPERIENCE

REECE

This is the most beautiful and simultaneously the most terrifying experience I've ever had in my life. All I can do at this moment is stare into my beautiful daughter's eyes and imagine the whole lifetime she has ahead of her.

I can't even describe the relief I'm feeling now that Rose is okay. She didn't seem too horrified that she'll never be able to have children again, but seeing how she just gave birth to four of them, and she's probably exhausted from the experience, it probably won't sink in for a while. After a little coaxing, the other Alphas and I finally got her to relax, and she's getting a little bit of rest right now.

In the meantime, we've all stepped into a separate room that Mark's pack has set up as a kind of nursery, with tiny little bassinets and several glider chairs—four larger ones for us Alphas and one smaller one that's perfect for Rose—and some soft, relaxing lighting.

I look up for a moment, and the other Alphas are still in the same mode I'm in. It's an almost indescribable mix of shock, pride, fear, happiness, and love. The books, and all the advice I'd gotten from pack mates who are already fathers were all correct—there's just no way to prepare for this experience.

A daughter—there's so much to think about now that I'm a father, and I don't even know where to start. I guess my immediate concern is how we're going to get her fed since she's got three brothers and sisters who all need their mother's milk, but it seems like the doctors and nurses here in Mark's pack have these things all under control.

I'm glad someone does.

Tristan speaks first. "Are the rest of you thinking the same thing I am?" he asks.

"I'm wondering how I'm going to teach him to be a fair, yet strong, leader," says Mark, looking proudly at his little son.

I laugh. "I've got, 'How many boys will I have to fight off?' over here," I say.

Everyone laughs at that, except Tristan, who gets wide-eyed and looks like he forgot to think about that. "Oh, great," he says. "One more thing to worry about."

"We're all going to worry for the rest of our lives," says Mark. "Everything changed forever the second these little ones came. But I think we can handle it."

"I'm looking at these bright red locks and thinking, 'Now I get to find out what my parents went through,'" says Eli.

Tristan chuckles. "That might be more trouble than mine over here," he says. "At least Reece has a girl, too. We can team up to fight off all those undesirables who think they're good enough for our little girls."

"Here, here," I say, pretending to raise an imaginary glass in a toast while careful not to change the baby's position. She looks comfortable, and I don't want to mess with success.

"I can't wait for Rose to wake up," says Mark. "We need to name these babies, but she gets first choice."

We all nod in agreement. "She did the hard part for sure," says Eli.

"So," says Tristan, "what exactly happened out there?" He looks at Eli and rearranges his daughter in his arms, brushing away her dark curls, which are surprisingly long for a newborn, I think, although I'm no expert. It looks like this will be my first and only child, and I'm perfectly content with that.

Eli rolls his eyes before he breaks into a long explanation about a group of rogues who took over some abandoned resort up in the mountains somewhere, how they ambushed their vehicles, and how two of his men had died in the crash. We're all silent for a few moments out of respect.

After a while, Tristan spoke again. "Must be a really old place," he says. "I've never heard of a resort anywhere around here."

"It looked relatively modern," says Eli. "Although that piece of shit van had way more miles than the poor thing could stand. I'm shocked that it got me close enough to reach you all."

"The Moon Goddess is definitely on our side in this one," says Mark. He smiles at his son and puts a finger on his tiny cheek.

The door opens, and Dr. Travesty walks in with a few nurses. I want to stand up but don't want to bother my precious daughter. No one else stands up either, so they all must be thinking the same thing.

"Rose?" asks Mark.

"She's fine," the doctor answers quickly. "But with so many babies born at once, we do need to give them a thorough check-up every so often, so we'll need those little ones now, one at a time."

She looks at me, and the last thing I want to do is hand my new baby daughter over to anyone, but I do it anyway, reluctantly. My arms feel so empty when the nurse takes her from me, and suddenly, a rush of dread comes over me as I wonder what it will be like when she gets married, and I have to say goodbye. What if she marries an Alpha from a distant pack? How will I ever live without her close to me?

The nurse looks at me with a polite smile, and almost as if she can read my mind, she says, "You'll get used to this, Alpha Reece. But I know how you feel. I remember when my little daughter was brand new. I didn't want her to leave my sight. But I promise, we'll just have her for a few minutes, then give her right back."

I nod and look over at the others, who I half-expect to be teasing me about it. But instead, the looks on their faces say that they're all suddenly terrified of handing their respective babies over to the nurses as well.

"I guess we're in this together," I say, chuckling a little at their expressions. "And that's a good thing. Most new fathers are on their own."

"True," says Mark.

"We'll make a good tag-team," says Tristan.

"For diaper changes?" asks Mark.

Tristan nods. "Oh, good Goddess," he says. "I hadn't even thought about that."

The nurses laugh at this one, and by then, they're done with my little girl and the same nurse hands her back to me carefully.

"She passed with flying colors," says Dr. Travesty.

The other Alphas give up their babies one by one, and thankfully, they all get a clean bill of health. But now, my little girl is starting to fuss, and it's scaring me.

"She's hungry," says the nurse. "For that, we'll need Miss Rose's expertise."

We all nod, and I can see that all the babies are starting to wiggle around a bit more, so we all try to compensate by bouncing them gently.

"We'll start with this little girl," says the doctor, nodding her head at me and my daughter. "Let's go see if Rose is up for nursing."

I follow the doctor around the corner to Rose's room, which is right next door to the nursery, and I'm happy to see that she's awake. She looks like the Goddess herself lying there practically glowing with happiness.

"How are you feeling, darlin'?" I ask her.

"Like I want to hold that little angel," she says, reaching out her hands.

I'm still a little awkward at this 'handling newborn pups' thing, but I manage the transfer successfully. Handing her to Rose is much easier than giving her to a nurse, and I sit down next to the bed while another nurse helps Rose reposition herself to feed the baby.

It's all a little awkward at first, and it really dawns on me that Rose is just as inexperienced in all this as I am—and she has the hardest part in it all. With a little help from the nurse, who clearly has a lot of experience in this sort of thing, unlike us, our little daughter is happily sucking away in no time.

We both just stare at her, mesmerized, her tiny little hand holding onto her mother while she eats. Rose's smile is bigger than a thousand suns, and I've got a grin I can't get off my face as well.

"I love you," I say in a whisper so as not to disturb our daughter.

Rose looks up at me, her eyes twinkling in the soft lighting. "I love you, too, Reece."

I lean in gently and give her a soft kiss, our lips lingering for just a moment before the baby starts moving around again.

The nurse walks up. "It looks like she's done for now," she says. "With three others in the wings, we'd better let them all get their turn with Mama."

"Mama," says Rose. "That's the most beautiful word."

"You're the most beautiful woman," I say.

She smiles wider, if that's possible, hands me back our daughter, and says, "What will we name her?"

"I think I'm going to let you decide that," I say. "The other Alphas agree."

Rose shakes her head. "No," she says. "I want us to decide as a family."

"Alright," I say. "I'm going to let the other babies and fathers have their moment for now. We'll talk about naming a bit later. I know the others were starting to get fussy."

"The babies or the Alphas?" she asks.

"Both," I joke. We both laugh and I kiss her once more before I head out the room. Yes, this is a beautiful experience.

CHAPTER 31: THAT DOCTOR IS A TRAVESTY

GENE

"The fucking Breeder had her babies?" I repeat to the servant who has just barged into my bathroom to give me this news. I am taking a soak in my garden tub, and the scents of roses, lilacs, and other flowers are wafting around me. I had found it soothing until a few moments ago when this idiot barged in.

"Yes, she did," he says, swallowing hard as he tries not to look directly at me. He's probably afraid he'll see my wee wee and never feel like a real man again. "We just got word from the castle, sir."

"What castle?" I ask. "You know a talking castle?"

I see him swallow again and wonder if he has something stuck in his throat. "No, sir. I mean… we got word from the spy you sent to Alpha Mark's castle, sir. He said that the breeder gave birth to four babies a little while ago, and that the Breeder herself almost died, but their doctor was able to bring her back."

I mull that information over. "The Breeder almost died of natural causes?" We almost got lucky enough to have the stupid bitch die on her own, but now I'll have to kill her.

"That's right. But she lived, thanks to the doctor, a Dr. Travesty." He gives a sharp nod.

"You're right. It is a doctor travesty that she was able to save her. Who was the doctor?"

"Dr. Travesty," he says.

"I agree wholeheartedly," I concur. "But what was her name?"

"Travesty, sir," he says again.

Now, I am starting to get irritated. "I do realize that it would've been better if the Breeder had died and the doctor hadn't saved her. That's why I'm asking who it was! So I can make sure they pay for committing this travesty against me. So, just tell me already! Who was the doctor who committed this travesty?"

"Yes, sir." His eyes are wide, and he keeps shuffling his feet, like I'm making him nervous.

"Yes, sir–what?" I scream, my hands splashing down in the water, causing some to spill over.

"Sir, it was Dr. Travesty. She saved the Breeder."

"Who saved the Breeder? Dr. who?"

"Dr. Travesty, sir!"

"Oh, all right then, don't fucking tell me!" I exclaim. "Go and fetch that man who used to work at Alpha Mark's castle. What's his name? Never mind. You probably don't know and we'll keep going in circles. Go!"

He turns around and takes off out of my bathroom like he's just seen something scary, and I have to imagine that it was my wee wee. It can be very intimidating because of its size.

Even though I'm not halfway done enjoying my soak, I decide it's time to get out so that I can speak to my new Beta about this situation. He already knows that he's been assigned to kill the Breeder, but if he knows she's had her pups already, things might change a bit for him. It would've been better for him to have killed her before they crawled out of her womb. Now, he'll have to kill them all individually, and that will be harder. While I imagine those pups won't be able to defend themselves very well, their Alpha fathers will be a tougher group to cut down.

I put on my robe and go out into my living quarters. When I open my closet doors, I do so quickly and have a look around, half expecting Luna Barbara to be there, but she's not. I am alone. I pick out a nice outfit to put on and am about to get dressed when there's a knock at the door.

Muttering under my breath about interruptions, I go to see who it is.

"You wanted to see me, Your Majesty?" a scrawny man with thick glasses and not much hair asks me. I feel sorry for him. He's so ugly. But then, not everyone can be as handsome as I am.

"Yes, you're the man from Alpha Mark's pack, aren't you?" I don't invite him inside. He can stand in the hallway.

"That's right, sir. Melvin."

"No, I'm King Gene!" I tell him, shaking my head. Everyone is so fucking stupid today. "What kind of a dumbass name is Melvin?"

He clears his throat. "No, Sir. That's my name."

"Oh. Well, anyway, I was just trying to figure out what happened with that Breeder at Mark's castle. I heard she almost died but then she was brought back to life by the pack doctor. Travesty."

"Yes, that's her," he replies with a nod.

I furrow my brows at him. "That's who?"

"The doctor. Travesty."

"Yes, it is a travesty. I'd be much happier if she'd died. But she didn't. So I want to make sure that she is killed as well as the doctor. So… do you know her name?"

"The doctor?" he asks me.

"Yes!" I'm starting to lose my patience again.

"Travesty," he says with a nod.

Taking a deep breath, I say, "I'm not asking for your opinion about the situation! I simply want to know her name!"

"But that is her name," he replies.

"What is her name? Butt?"

"But what?"

"I don't know!" I shout at him. "Just tell me the doctor's fucking name!"

Beads of sweat pop up on his forehead as he looks at me behind those thick frames. "Dr. Travesty, sir. That's her name. That's what her name is."

"Her name is That?" I ask, finally starting to think I understand.

"Yes. That's right," he says, looking slightly less frightened.

"Well, why didn't you say That to begin with?" I ask him.

He shakes his head slowly. "I'm sorry, sir. I thought I did say that."

"All right, all right," I tell him, waving him away. I'm done with him now. No need to continue to shout at him. "You can go. But next time, be more clear, won't you?"

"Yes, sir. I'm sorry about that." He takes a few steps away from me, backing down the hallway.

"I'm sorry about That, too." And I truly am. "That really is a travesty."

He says nothing, but I see his brows furrow, and rather than going through it again, I shut the door.

Through the mind-link, I contact my new Beta. 'Listen, I'm giving you a new assignment,' I tell him. 'When you go to kill the Breeder and her pups, you'll need to add another person to the list. The doctor who delivered the pups.'

A second later, his voice fills my head. 'Which doctor is that?'

'Precisely.'

CHAPTER 32: GET US OUT OF HERE

Eli

Tristan, Mark, and Reece have all spent some time with Rose now, and we've taken a few turns going in so Rose can feed the pups. They all look so full and satisfied, sleeping in their little bassinets with nurses coming and going quietly, and Rose is resting again now. I can't imagine what it must be like to give birth to four pups at the same time, so we're going to give her all the rest time she needs.

I don't want to take my eyes off my new little son. He looks so perfect, lying there with his little tufts of red hair sticking out of his little knit cap. His hands are so tiny, and so are his little toes—how could anything be so tiny and beautiful?

I have to chuckle a little when I look at that red hair—it looks just like mine. I remember when I was younger. Back then, I hated my red hair because it made me stick out in the crowd. As the Alpha's son, I was always meant to be his heir, but it seemed to make people jealous that I was different from them. I guess no kid wants to feel that they don't fit in, even if it's because they're the future Alpha.

In my case, all this red comes mostly from my mother, who had long, curly, bright red hair, while my father just had a bit of red showing when the sunlight hit him just right. Mom had a red wolf, and everyone respected her as a great Luna, and Dad's wolf had dark black fur that, like his hair, shined with glittering red in the sun.

I wonder whether my son will have a red wolf, just like me. And I'll make sure that he knows how it makes him special, and that it's okay to be a little different.

Reece taps me on the shoulder and makes a nodding motion toward the door. I hadn't even noticed that anyone had stood up, but the rest of the Alphas are already walking out. They all look just as reluctant as I am to leave the pups behind in their little bassinets.

"They'll be fine," says Tristan once we're out in the hallway. "I trust Mark's people to take care of them, as much as I don't want to leave my little mini flower. But it's been a long night, and we're no good to Rose on empty stomachs."

I hadn't even noticed it until now, but I am feeling hungry. I guess the whole night passed between the births of all four babies, and it's already time for breakfast. I'd been so focused on my son and Rose that I'd forgotten to even tell Kelly about my little pup, but I'm sure Mark's people have made my sister comfortable somewhere and have updated her on all the news.

I'm surprised she hasn't mind-linked me yet, but she probably wants me to enjoy my new role as a father.

'Kelly?' I say in the mind-link, focusing on her. She doesn't answer, and it's not like her to ignore me, so maybe she's still asleep. It is pretty early, I suppose, and we had a late night.

Mark's chef has a full spread ready for us in the dining hall, and it's definitely a breakfast fit for an Alpha. We walk in and everyone greets Mark warmly, so he has to stop at a few tables to shake some hands and say his thanks for their congratulations. It isn't every day a pack welcomes a new Alpha heir.

Everyone is also congratulating the rest of us, so Reece, Tristan, and I also find ourselves shaking a bunch of hands of people we don't know. The women are all excited to meet Rose and to see the pups, and we have to explain that it might take a few days since they're so tiny. Everyone seems to understand, and they're so friendly.

Well, almost everyone is friendly. There's a table over in the far corner of the room, and I notice that everyone sitting at it looks gloomy and grumpy, especially this one big guy wearing overalls and a white T-shirt, which I find a little strange because everyone else is dressed a bit more formally.

The servants show me to a seat next to Mark, so I lean over and ask, "What's up with that guy?" I try to casually nod over toward the corner table in a way no one will notice, but when I look up, the big guy is glaring at me. I glare right back, and he finally averts his eyes.

"That's Al," says Mark. "His father was once Beta to my father, but he's always been mad that I didn't make him my Beta. I would have if he were qualified, but he has no respect for the position, so I chose someone else. He thinks that somehow, he should go straight from Beta's son to Alpha, so I suppose he's a little more grumpy today now that I have an heir."

"Got it," I say. "Is he a threat?"

Mark shakes his head. "He hasn't been a problem," he says. "He's all about complaining but doesn't have the teeth to back it up. I'm not worried about Al."

"Still," I say, "I'll keep my eye on him."

Mark nods with a lighthearted laugh and digs into the huge plate of bacon in front of him. I join him; I was hungry before, but the smell of all this incredible food is making me not want to mind my table manners.

I'm taking a bite that's a perfect mix of scrambled eggs, bacon, and ham when I look up and notice a woman coming through the cafeteria door. I can read the worry on her face, and for some reason, it starts to worry me, too.

Within seconds, she's running up to Mark. "Alpha Mark," she says, taking a quick second to make the sign of respect. "My mate Chris… he never came home last night! Do you know where he is? He's not answering my mind-link either. Something… something's wrong!"

I have no idea who Chris is, but a strange feeling runs through my spine. I don't like this.

Mark looks at me. "Where's Kelly?" he asks.

"I have no idea," I say. "I guess she's still asleep?"

Mark pushes his chair back, stands up, and shouts, "Vicky!"

A middle-aged woman appears from the kitchen. "Yes, Alpha Mark?" she says.

"Our guests… where did you put them?" asks Mark.

"Guests?" Vicky asks. "We readied some rooms, but only Alpha Eli here arrived. We assumed that—"

Mark flipped his gaze over to me. "Kelly…" he says.

I'm already frantically trying to reach her in the mind-link, but I get nothing. I shake my head and push away from the table myself.

I'm not very hungry anymore.

KELLY

I'm still struggling to see with the blinding light in my face, but I do sense that someone has entered the room and shoved something in my hand. Whatever it is, it smells good, and it makes my stomach growl after who knows how long that I've been trapped… wherever this is.

As my eyes adjust, I see that it's a woman. She's wearing what used to be a dress but is now just a torn, thread-bare pile of rags. Her face is dirty and so is her hair… looking closer, I see that she's not a woman but a girl, probably younger than Heather.

For the first time, I can see Heather across from me, and the girl who had entered the room is putting something in her hand, too. Then she pulls out what looks like a couple of bottles of water from a bag she's carrying, and she hands those to each of us as well.

Heather looks terrified but calm. She's sitting on the floor, like I am, her eyes still blinking as she tries to adjust to this new flood of lighting herself. I try to mouth the words to her that it's okay, but I really know that it's not okay, not at all.

We're both chained to the wall in some weird dungeon-like place with dirt floors and what looks like a huge steel door, which the girl now steps through and closes, leaving us behind without a word.

"It's… it's bread," says Heather quietly. "Do you think it's safe to eat? I'm starving."

For the first time, I turn my attention to the lump in my hand, which I now recognize as some sort of a dinner roll. It's not much, but the smell and the proximity of it make me want to inhale it. But, like Heather, I know to use caution.

What in the world had Heather gone through in her life to make her so calm right now?

"I don't know," I say. "Let me try it first, and we'll give it a few minutes. Then if it's okay, you can eat it."

"Okay," she says.

I guess if they—whoever 'they' are—are going to poison us, then I'd rather they do it to me first. It's not like we have a choice. We're going to have to eat eventually. But why are they keeping us here, and why are they feeding us?

A few moments after I take my first bite, I give the go-ahead to Heather. I know she can't hold back much longer. It's a little hard to eat with the position our hands are in with the chains, but I manage, and then I manage to open the water bottle, which is sealed, and I'm glad of that. It likely hasn't been tampered with.

"I wish it weren't so dark in here," Heather says. "Will we ever get out of here, Kelly?"

"We're going to try," I tell her. "We're certainly going to try."

CHAPTER 33: NOT THE BETA ANYMORE

Adam

Alastor Dravenwolf has left the castle, and I don't think this is a good thing. In fact, it makes me very nervous.

The new Beta that Alpha King Gene has just named to replace me looks a bit deranged to me, and I wouldn't be surprised if he hasn't actually been diagnosed with something like... being a fucking psychopath. Is that a diagnosis one can get and still be allowed to wander about freely?

I need to figure out where he's gone and chase him down. I've decided to gather together all of the forces that are technically part of the king's guard but are more loyal to me and take them with me. Alastor took a small number of troops with him when he left, headed toward Alpha Mark's castle, so I know I'll have to have some troops with me or else I will be greatly outnumbered.

The only problem is, asking these soldiers to go against the king is technically insurrection. That would make me a traitor, and if I'm caught, the punishment is death. I'm certain that Alpha King Gene will not hesitate one moment to put me to death either since he's already demoted me from my position as Beta. He clearly doesn't value me right now, and I guess I shouldn't blame him since I am now acting against him.

"It's too dangerous," Shelby is saying, her arms folded. "I don't think we should be doing this. I think you should just contact the Alphas and let them know that Alastor is on the way to the castle to murder all of them."

I look at her, trying not to sigh. "That's not enough, Shelby. They are all busy right now with the babies and Rose. I have to go there myself. Besides, what's the point in staying here when Gene no longer appreciates me anyway? He's likely to come after both of us. That's why I want you to go to your mother's for a bit."

She shakes her head. "I'm not doing that, Adam. I'm coming with you."

"Absolutely not!" I tell her, taking her by the upper arms so she has to look at me. "It's far too dangerous, what I'm about to do. I can't have you hurt in battle or put to death by King Gene for being a traitor like me."

"I'm not asking your permission, Adam!" she declares, wiggling free of me. "We are in this together! Where you go, I go!"

"That doesn't include the battlefield, Shelby. You're not trained to be out there." I hope she can see reason, but her expression tells me that she isn't listening to me.

"I have trained to fight, just like every wolf in my pack, and I will be just fine out there. Besides, even if the worst happens, I'd rather be out there with you, dying alongside you, than sitting back here trying to dodge Gene or going to my mother's and sitting there wondering if you are okay or bothering you over the mind-link every five seconds to make sure that you're alive!"

"You'd rather just watch me die on the battlefield in person?" I ask her, and I'm only half teasing.

She narrows her eyes at me and folds her arms beneath her chest. Clearly, my wife doesn't think jokes about me dying are funny. "No, but if you're not careful, you'll be dying right here."

I chuckle, but something tells me she's not actually joking.

"Adam, I'm coming with you. If you don't like it, that's too fucking bad."

Her seriousness is noted in her eyes, and I decide it's a waste of valuable time for me to continue to argue with her.

"Fine. But you stay near the back, and don't do anything stupid," I tell her.

Shelby scoffs. "When have I ever done anything stupid?"

I know she literally will kill me if I am stupid enough to answer that question. "Okay," is all I say to her, and I go about preparing myself to go make an argument to the people I think will join us. I am terrified, though. It only takes one of them to turn on me and arrest me, throwing me in prison, and then... everything could be over for all of us.

Before I leave to go to the barracks where the guards spend their free time, I send out a mind-link message, deciding it would be best to just warn one of the Alphas, and since it's Mark's castle Alastor is headed to, I choose him.

'Alpha Mark,' I tell him, waiting for him to acknowledge me before I continue.

'Not now, Adam. We have a crisis on our hands here at the castle,' he says, his voice showing his strain, even through the mind-link.

'Oh, you already know, then? Does that mean he's arrived?' I ask, not wanting to be completely deterred by his dismissive statement in case we are not talking about the same thing.

'Who has arrived at the castle?' he asks me.

'Alastor Dravenwolf, Gene's new Beta. He's leading a force to the castle to attack and kill all of you.'

He is quiet for a moment, and I start to think perhaps he hasn't heard me, but then he asks, 'King Gene has a new Beta? And he's coming to my castle to kill all of us?'

'That's right,' I tell him. 'He left about thirty minutes ago. On foot.'

'Fuck,' Mark mumbles. 'Now is really not a good time.'

I'm not sure how to respond to that. It's not as if I have had anything to do with it, though I suppose I could have warned him earlier. I intended to, but the situation here at the castle keeps changing, and it took Beta Alastor a while to get his troops together to march on Mark's castle since most of the soldiers in Gene's army have been used to swearing allegiance to the Alphas and don't want to fight them.

'I'm planning on leading a force from here and going after him,' I explain to Alpha Mark. 'But I thought that you should be aware of the situation so that you can prepare your own army.'

'And how many troops do you think Alastor has with him?' he asks me.

'I'm not sure,' I admit. 'But it didn't look like a big force. I believe he thinks he can order you all to come with him or somehow sneak into the castle and take you out that way. I think that Gene may have some people working for him amongst your staff.'

'My staff?' I hear the doubt in his voice. 'No. All of my staff members are completely loyal to me.'

'Uhm… no disrespect intended, Alpha, but are you sure about that? I mean, Gene has received some information recently regarding the situation in the castle that he couldn't have possibly known unless someone there was talking to him. He even knows the name of the doctor that delivered the pups.' I hope that he will listen to me because I am about out of patience and time.

'All right. I'll look into it,' he says. 'But it may take me a while. We'll be ready for Alastor to arrive, but we need to focus on the other matter at hand right now.'

'What other matter at hand?' I ask him, thinking he might be talking about Rose and the pups.

So I'm shocked when he says, 'Finding Kelly.'

CHAPTER 34: OVER MY COLD, DEAD BODY

Mark

"We have a problem," I say.

We're standing in the hallway outside the nursery and Rose's room. The other three Alphas are looking at me like I'm crazy, because of course we have a problem with Kelly missing… along with a loyal member of my pack. But from what Adam just told me, we have a lot more to worry about.

"What now?" Tristan asks after staring at me for a moment with an exasperated look.

"We can't leave," I say.

"What?" asks Eli. "But my sister—"

I hold up my hand. "I know," I say. "We need to figure out what's happened with Kelly. But there's a greater danger for Rose and the pups right now."

Tristan bolts right off without another word and runs into the room where the babies are sleeping, pretty much waking them up. I wave him back as the nurses give him irritated glances. Satisfied that all the pups are fine, he comes to his senses and exits, closing the door quietly and walking back over to us. Now he's the one looking irritated.

"I didn't mean right this second," I say. "But I understand how you're feeling. We're all a bit jumpy with even more at stake now. But listen. Adam says that Gene fired him and replaced him with another Beta who's—"

"What?!" This time it is Reece getting upset.

I nod and continue. "Who is this very moment marching here to kill us all—Rose, the pups, us."

"Over my cold, dead body!" hollers Tristan.

I feel the same way, but I look over at the nurse who's just put her hand on the doorknob to the pups' room. Something looks off about her. I know everyone in my pack, and she doesn't look familiar, and she's averting her eyes. "Excuse me...."

She turns and looks at me with wide eyes and starts backing away.

"Stop," I say in my Alpha voice. She does just that, and I can feel the eyes of the rest of the Alphas, who immediately sense that something is wrong.

"We're moving the pups," says Reece without waiting to see what's wrong or what will happen next. "Pups and Rose in the same room, and one or more of us will be there at all times."

Everyone is murmuring in agreement as I hold the nurse by the arm and open the nursery door, indicating to the other nurses inside that they should come out into the hallway.

"Does anyone know this woman?" I ask when they're standing around me.

They all shake their heads, and their eyes go wide as they realize that the strange woman is wearing a nurse's uniform.

"Never seen her before, Alpha," says one of the older nurses. "I assumed she was from another pack."

It angers me a bit that she'd make such an assumption about a stranger who has access to the pups, but there's never been a danger inside my castle walls, so I don't blame her for being trusting. "From now on, we'll be restricting access to the pups to only our best head nurses," I say. "Create an identification procedure, and no one else is allowed near the pups or Rose. And get them all in the same room as Alpha Reece has ordered."

"Yes, Alpha," says the nurse, and she turns to get started right away.

The guards I'd called in the mind-link arrive. "Detain this woman," I say.

Tristan moves in very closely so that he's right in her face, which must be more than intimidating considering his body size and Alpha status. "Who do you work for?"

She looked up at him, terrified.

"Answer the Alpha's question," I say firmly.

"He... he said we'd all starve!" she says.

"That's not an answer," says Tristan, and I have to say that even I would answer him right now with the way his eyes are flaming.

"Al," she says. "Al says that if the three other Alphas along with the pups take over, that they... that you'd hoard all the food, and we'd all starve!"

"Why the hell would we do something like that?" asks Reece, and that's exactly what I'm about to ask.

"I'd better go check in on Rose and explain why the pups are moving in," says Eli, and he heads over to Rose's room. I hadn't even noticed the bustle of nurses rolling by bassinets and equipment and carrying pups toward Rose's room, so I'm glad Eli is paying attention. Rose is probably confused... or terrified.

"I... we all remember Alpha Trevor," says the nurse that we're questioning.

And now it makes sense.

"Alpha Trevor has been dead for two centuries!" I say. "All we've ever heard of him is childhood stories."

"Who the fuck is Alpha Trevor?" asks Tristan.

I realize that the other Alphas have no knowledge of my pack's history. In fact, we really know very little about each other or each other's packs, which is odd considering that we all just had pups born of the same beautiful woman. "It's a long story," I say. "But it's an old one that has nothing to do with anything that's happening right now. Alpha Trevor had triplet sons. He was also a hell of a mean bastard. When his sons were still infants, he divided the pack into three and made each section pay 'tribute' to a different son. That meant most of the money, products, produce, and meat went directly to him. That left most of the pack in starvation mode for decades. And when his sons grew up and tried to take over from him, he had them killed and still kept everything for himself."

"What the hell?" says Tristan.

I shrugged. "I guess the multiple birth has a few of my people nervous. But what they've forgotten," I say while turning back to the frightened fake nurse, "is that it was my family who stood up to the bastard and set things right. Why the hell would I be like Alpha Trevor? Have you ever known me to rule like Alpha Trevor?"

She shook her head. "It's just that… well, Al sounded convincing. He said it didn't matter what your ancestors did because you'd take the birth of all these pups and forget about the good your family had done because you'd want everything for you and the pups now."

"And you honestly believed that?" I ask. I don't usually use the word 'flabbergasted,' but that's exactly how I feel right now. "These aren't even all my pups. We have three other Alpha fathers here." In my mind-link, I contact another set of guards and have them arrest Al and anyone around him. He has to be the one who's been leaking information to Gene.

I'd never felt unsafe in my own castle before… until now. "Get her out of here," I say to the guards, and they haul her away to the dungeon, which I don't even think has anyone in it right now. Well, it will now. It'll be full of anyone connected to Al and his stupid ideas about me. I block all of them from making any mind-link communications with each other or anyone else.

By now, it looks like all the pups have been moved into Rose's room, so Tristan, Reece, and I head inside. Eli is sitting next to her bed holding his son, and Rose looks worried.

"What's going on?" she says. "Eli says we have to keep the pups and me in the same room due to a threat. What's the threat?"

I really don't want to scare Rose since she has enough to worry about with healing up and caring for the pups, but she's a strong woman, and she has a right to be a part of our decisions. "Apparently,

I have a few people in my pack who remember an awful leader of the past, and they think that just because you've had a multiple birth that I'm going to do the same terrible things that asshole did."

"His Luna had four babies?" she asks.

"Three," I say. "But I guess old fears die hard, and bad people can use them to get other people to follow them, apparently."

Tristan nods. "So now we have three issues to deal with," he says.

"Three issues?" asks Rose.

I nod. "Yes," I say. "One, I've got an internal problem that could be causing a leak of information. I'll deal with that myself. Two, we need to find Kelly—"

"What's wrong with Kelly?!" Rose sits up straight in her bed and looks between all of us with a furrowed brow.

"Apparently, she didn't make it back like Eli did," I say. "She was in a different vehicle."

Her mouth goes wide, and she turns back to Eli. "Why didn't you tell me?" she says.

"I didn't want to worry you," he says. "You need to heal and care for the pups. I'll find my sister."

"Well, go!" she says, spreading out her arms to take her son.

"I agree," says Tristan. "If you take a contingent to go find Kelly, and Mark deals with the issue with his pack, that leaves me and Reece to guard Rose. I've already got half my army outside, and the other half is dealing with logistics and will be here soon."

"My army is here as well," says Reece. "Guarding the outskirts."

"Wait," says Rose. "Why all this guarding? What's going on that you haven't told me? There's a third issue...."

We all look at each other, but I speak up first.

"Gene has sent warriors to kill us all."

CHAPTER 35: NAMING THE PUPS

R̶ose

Mark's words hammer around in my head for a moment as I try to process what he's saying to me.

King Gene has sent his warriors to kill us all.

Ordinarily, I would laugh at something like that. It's not as if Gene has any warriors I'm actually afraid of. He is a bumbling idiot who can't even tie his own shoes, so I would seriously doubt him capable of doing anything that was going to truly harm me or my children.

But that's just it. I look around the room and see their little faces, all of them sleeping except for Tristan's daughter who is looking at me like I'm a snack, probably because I am to her, and that baby eats almost as much as her father, but the fact that my babies are here now, I can see them and touch them with my hands, that makes me nervous.

"Wh-what do you mean?" I ask Mark, my voice quivering with each word.

"Goddessfuckingdamnit, Mark!" Tristan says, shaking his head at the other Alpha, his hands set on his hips in fists. "Why do you have to be so fucking blunt?"

Mark's eyes widen slightly. "She deserves to know what's going on with our pups!"

"Sure, she deserves to know, but you don't have to tell her like it's the end of the fucking world!" Tristan shouts, and I know that we are all about at the end of our ropes. It's been a stressful few days–weeks, maybe even months–and we are beginning to lose patience with one another.

Reece steps in, his tone calm as he begins to explain to me. "It's Gene, darlin', so we all know there's really nothing to be too worried about. It's only that he's got some new guy he thinks is stronger than all of us, and he's sending him to stir up some trouble. Believe me, just like all of Alpha King Gene's men, this guy is no great match for us. We'll be able to take him out with absolutely no problem. All you need to do is worry about getting some rest and feeding these pups when they start asking for mama."

Even as Reece is speaking, Tristan's daughter begins to fuss. I don't like thinking of her only as his kid. She needs a name. They all do.

"Guys, before you take off, and I know it's important that you get to Kelly as soon as you can, Eli, I think... we should name these babies."

"We were going to leave that up to you, beautiful," Eli says to me. I can tell he's distracted and wants to go, and I don't blame him. Kelly is one of my best friends, and if anything ever happened to her, I'd be beside myself. I hope she's just lost in the woods somewhere....

"Okay," I say, seeing that they're all nodding at me. "Well, I would like for each baby to have a name similar to each of you so that there's no question who their fathers are. So... I was thinking, for Tristan's daughter, Trisha."

"Oh, I like that," Tristan says with a smile as he gazes down at his curly headed daughter. She's already sucking her fist. "What do you think? Do you like Trisha?"

"Can we call her Trish for short?" Reece asks, snickering, and Tristan, who hates being called Trist, glares at him.

"No, no you may not," he says. He scoops her up as she begins to grunt and hands her to me to feed. Tristan bends down and kisses me quickly, and I know now that this little glutton of a pup is my sweet Trisha.

As I latch her on to feed, I say, "The other girl, Reece, your daughter, I think we should call Reeva."

"Reeva?" he repeats, his eyes beginning to glisten with tears. "I love it!" His daughter is still sleeping, but he pats her chest softly, and she sticks her tongue out.

"Eli, how about Ethan for your son?"

He nods and cracks a smile. "Yeah, that's great. Can his middle name be Kenny, for Kelly?"

"I like that," I tell him, thinking now they will all need middle names. Naming this many babies is hard….

"Mark, I've had a hard time coming up with a name that is similar to yours for your son. I know it's not too similar, but what about… Matthew?"

"Matthew?" When he repeats the name, he doesn't react at all, and I'm afraid he hates it.

"He'll be the next king, right after you," Tristan reminds the other Alpha, and he has a point. By King Gene's decree, not only is Alpha Mark supposed to be the new king since his son was born first, his child is heir to the throne.

"Alpha King Matthew?" Mark says again. "Okay. Yeah. Let's go with that." He is nodding and seems to like the name, and I relax a little, glad that I have finally got names for all of my children.

"All right, you guys," I say. "Go ahead and go save the world, but be careful."

"Don't worry. Reece and I will be right here," Tristan assures me.

Reece leans over and kisses me. "We won't let anything bad happen to you or our babies," he says, and I believe him.

Eli comes over and kisses me deeply. "We'll find Kelly," he says. "I've already assembled my team."

Mark is the last to kiss me, and he takes his time. It isn't until Tristan says, "You do know my daughter is watching, right?" that Mark lets up.

Mark glares at him and then says, "I'll be back as soon as I interrogate these traitors." He has his Alpha face on now, and I would feel sorry for anyone who crossed his path if they didn't deserve to be punished for what they've done.

As two of my men leave, the other two sit down in rocking chairs the nurses have moved in. Trisha is about full, I think, but before long, someone else will wake up and want to eat. I am amazed that my body has the power to create enough milk to feed all of my babies, but then, I had a magical body that was able to create all of these babies to begin with, so why should I be surprised.

"We did have some DNA tests done, just to be sure, and we are all right about which baby is which," Reece explains to me.

It hadn't even crossed my mind to do such a thing since I knew from the moment I saw each of my children's faces who their fathers were, but that makes me happy.

Despite all of the chaos going on around me, I tilt my head back and reach for sleep. I am worried about Kelly, but that's the only thing I'm worried about now. I know I'm safe and so are my babies.

My Alphas will never fail us….

CHAPTER 36: A CHANCE AT FREEDOM

SHELBY

There's no way I'm letting Adam run off after that new Beta and his goons without me. I know he wants to protect me, but we're all trained to fight, and I can hold my own well enough.

I'm really impressed with him right now as I sit beside him in the SUV. That Dravenwolf asshole took half the vehicles and equipment, so we're headed out in the other half with as much equipment as we can carry. Adam had decided that it was better to be well-armed than to shift and try to take on the enemy in our wolf forms.

Adam looks so determined right now, so regal—and it's sexy.

Adam was trained to take over as Beta from a very young age, so he's really good at looking the part. He's sitting here staring straight ahead, a serious but relaxed look on his face. But I know him better than anyone else, and I know what's going on under that calm, cool exterior.

He's afraid.

Adam is no coward, so I don't think he's afraid for himself. No, he's afraid for Rose, and for the pups, and for Kelly… Goddess, I hope Kelly is okay.

'None of this is your fault,' I say in a private mind-link. There's a driver and another warrior in the front seat, and I don't want to broadcast Adam's private feelings to the world. I just want to make him feel better.

'I know,' he answers in my mind, but the expression on his face tells me that he isn't so sure.

'Your job was to serve the Alpha King, and you did so honorably,' I say. 'It's not your fault that he was really a lying, scheming asshole, or that his mind is now deteriorating to the point where other bad people can take advantage of that.'

'My job....'

He has a faraway look on his face as he says the words in my mind. Losing his position is hitting him hard.

'Your job still exists,' I say. 'The new Alpha King will need a Beta.'

'True, but all these Alphas have their own Betas,' he says. 'Don't you think they'll bring them to the castle to rule with them? I'm telling you, there's nothing left here for me.'

I pierce my lips together and take a deep breath. 'Me,' I tell him. 'I'm left.'

He turns to look at me, and I think I see tears welling up in his eyes.

'Wherever you are and whatever you do, I'm with you,' I say, still in the mind-link but squeezing his hand.

'You're very sexy when you're loyal and noble,' he tells me with a little smirk on his face. The tears are still there, but at least his face has brightened up a bit.

'Right back at you,' I tell him. 'But I don't think we should start anything like that right now.'

He looks up at the men in the front seat and grunts a little. I can't help but giggle, although I'd really prefer that we be alone right now, too. It's so hard to break off the attraction with a mate. Once we get started, it takes everything we have to stop it and not rip each other's clothes off right then and there.

The slowing of the vehicle snaps me out of my thoughts. "What's happening?" I ask out loud. I guess getting back to reality is one way to cool the heat.

"I don't know," Adam says, and I can tell he's talking to others in the mind-link, but he's definitely leaving me out of the conversation this time. This can't be good.

"Adam, what's wrong?" I ask with a little bit of snap to my voice.

"There's something up ahead," he says. "Or... someone."

"What do you mean?" I ask, but the way his eyes look, I don't think I really want to know the answer.

"There's a dead body up ahead," he says quietly.

KELLY

"Look. We're obviously trapped here, and we're going to stay put. Why not at least unchain us... please?" I've lost track of how many times this young girl in the tattered clothes has come to feed us, and she still hasn't said a word. But sitting here in this position with my arms chained awkwardly above my head is starting to make my hands go numb.

Goddess, I'd give anything to be able to shift.

But I still feel a force of some kind preventing just that. And no one is answering my mind-links. Either I'm out of range or a strong Alpha is nearby blocking me.

And frankly, I'm pretty pissed, not just for me but for Heather, and for this other young girl who obviously is being mistreated and ignored while being forced to care for us. The food she's given us so far is really good, and the water is fresh. But this girl... she looks like she hasn't had a decent meal in years.

I just don't understand what's going on.

"Can you at least tell me your name?" I ask the girl.

She pauses at the door, which she was about to exit, and takes a deep breath. I sense quite a bit of hesitancy in her; I can hear her speeding heartbeat. She's afraid of someone, but she's considering my offer. I don't want to get her into trouble, but I don't think Heather and I can stand much more time chained up like this.

"Kara," she says in a whisper, or at least that's what I think she says.

"Kara?" I ask.

She nods and turns around. "Yes, I'm Kara," she says. "I'm not supposed to talk to you."

"I imagine not," I say. "But I can tell that you're a good person. I can tell you don't want to treat us this way, and that you don't want these people—whoever they are—to treat you badly, either. Are they treating you badly?"

Her eyes widen. "How... how did you know?" she asks.

I'm getting through to her. I might have the chance now to save both Kara and Heather... and myself. I soften my voice. "Because you look mistreated," I say. "When's the last time you had a good meal?"

She shrugs, and her whole demeanor seems resigned to her fate, as though she'd given up hope of being in a better situation long ago. "I eat okay," she says.

"I don't think you do," I say. "And I want to help. I'll make you a deal. You unhook these chains for us, and if we see anyone else come in here, we'll lock ourselves back up quickly so no one will know you did it."

"I... I don't know," she says. "Besides, I don't have the key."

"Do you know who has it?" asks Heather.

I look over at Heather, and her expression is full of hope. I think we'll be able to get Kara on our side, but I'm going to have to be careful. I don't want to put her—or Heather—into any more danger than they're already in.

"He does," Kara says.

"Who's 'he'?" asks Heather.

Kara shakes her head. "I don't know his name," she says. "And I'm not allowed to ask."

"Okay," I say. "Kara, I'm going to ask you to do me a big favor. But I want you to be very careful, because I don't want anyone to hurt you. Okay?"

She nods.

"Whoever this man is, do you ever see him asleep?" I ask.

"Sometimes," she says with a shrug.

"Okay, that's good," I say. "Now, the next time he's asleep, do you think you can get the keys from him? I need you to do it very carefully and to make sure that he doesn't wake up. If he starts to wake up, I want you to pretend you just tripped or something and just don't grab for the keys. But if he keeps sleeping, take the keys quietly."

"I... I think I can do that," she says.

"Okay," I say. "Now remember, you have to be very careful. If you can do that, when people come to rescue me and Heather here, we can help you, too."

"Heather," she says. "That's a pretty name."

The girls smile at each other, and for the first time since I've been in this cave—or whatever it is—I'm starting to feel hopeful.

"I have to go," she says. "I'll try."

"That's all you can do," I say. "Thank you, Kara."

She nods and exits the huge steel door, and I hear the clank of the lock from the other side.

"Do you think she can do it?" asks Heather.

I can't see her anymore in the darkness, but I can sense that she feels optimistic, too. "I hope so," I say. "I really hope so."

CHAPTER 37: WHO ARE YOU?

"I'm telling you, I don't know about the woman nurse!" Al says, spitting blood out of his mouth onto the concrete floor of the dungeon.

I've always taken great pride in my dungeon floor being pretty clean, so I don't appreciate it, but it's not as if I can fully blame him.

I'm the one who has been punching him until his mouth bleeds, after all.

"She said you told her that I was going to starve the pack and take away all of the nice things that everyone enjoys in our pack lands because I'll want it all for my baby, like that Alpha of old. She said you were the one spreading all of that information." My fists are aching from the last time I punched him, but I am longing to do it again. I need to know who else might be working with him so that I can prevent any more mayhem from unfolding.

Al shakes his head, giving me a devilish grin. "I can see fear in your eyes, Alpha. It's too bad you didn't choose me to be your Beta, ain't it? I coulda made sure that no one was able to hurt your pups."

Even the words "hurt" and "pups" coming out of his mouth at the same time had me punching him again. I punch him so hard, his head hits the wall, and his eyes roll back into his head.

He's unconscious.

"Fuck," I mumble. I'm upset that I'd knocked him out without getting an answer.

And now I have no reason to keep punching him, which is perhaps the most irritating of all.

Just when I have given up any hope of getting to crush his skull some more, I look up to see one of my guards coming down the stairs, and the thought of it falls from my mind anyway.

That wasn't me....

"Alpha, there's a young woman here to speak to you. She says she's from Miss Rose's pack, sent by her parents." The guard looks at me with hesitation on his face, as if he's afraid I might explode at him.

My people are not used to seeing me this angry–and dripping with blood, not the ones who work in the castle, anyway. The warriors, of course, but not these people.

"Where is she?" I ask him. I'm leery of letting anyone walk into the castle at the moment since Al has nothing to tell me, and the nurse who'd been working with the babies doesn't know anything she hasn't already told us.

She is still spending time in the prison anyway, though, for conspiring against Rose, the babies, and me.

"She's in the library, sir." He hurries away from me like I'm about to pound him, too.

I head up to the first floor of the castle and stop in a powder room to wash the blood off of my hands and see it has sprayed across my face as well. No wonder the guard who came to speak to me had looked at me like he was frightened.

I wash my face as well and then make my way to the room where the woman was waiting.

She isn't what I'm expecting.

I walk in to find a young woman, probably about Rose's age, with dark, curly hair, and a pleasant smile.

She stands and bows at the waist. "Sir," she says, "Alpha Mark. It's so nice to meet you." Extending her hand, she says, "I'm Retta. Rose's parents sent me."

I take her hand and shake it, offering for her to reclaim her seat as I sit across from her. "I hope you'll forgive my abruptness, miss," I tell her, "but we've had some problems here at the castle with people trying to sneak in who shouldn't be here."

"Oh, no," she says. "I'm very sorry to hear that. Well, I can assure you that Rose's parents sent me, and they can confirm that over the phone, if you'd like. Also, Rose knows me. We went to school together."

I arch an eyebrow at her. "That's odd. Rose never mentioned you before. The two of you were friends?"

Her face reddens as she shakes her head. "No, I wouldn't say that. Rose was the Alpha's daughter, so it was a bit difficult for most of us to approach her. What with her being… so beautiful, and in a different social class than us, and all of that. I wanted to be friends with her, but I didn't think I was worthy."

What she is saying seems believable to me, so far. "Why are you here, exactly? Just a representative from your pack?"

"No, Alpha, sir. On the contrary. I'm here because my Alpha and Luna wanted someone they could trust to keep an eye on the babies, and because I am now a trained pack healer. I hope that I can be of assistance to Miss Rose and the pups." She smiles prettily at me, and I feel like perhaps I can believe her.

But there is only one way to tell.

"I suppose I can take you to Rose, and she can let me know whether or not she wants you to stay. It's not as if she and her parents get along."

Her eyebrows furrow. "No, I didn't realize that, but that's very sad. I had no idea she was having trouble with her parents."

That makes me arch both of my brows. "Really?"

She shrugs. "Well, the family always put on a united front, you know? They wouldn't want anyone to know if they weren't getting along."

That makes sense to me as well.

I have a lot of important matters to tend to, especially now that I suspect there are more spies in our midst. "I'll take you to Miss Rose," I tell her. Standing, I gesture for her to follow me, and then I head to the room where Rose and the pups are.

She's asleep, with Tristan resting in a chair on one side of her and Reece holding his daughter on the other side, rocking her.

The moment we enter, Tristan is fully awake. "Who is she?" he barks, waking Rose.

"She's from Rose's parents' pack," I explain. "At least... she claims to be. Rose, do you know her?" I ask.

Rose stares at Retta long and hard before she says, "Yes, I know her all right."

I hold my breath. Maybe I shouldn't have brought the woman here after all.

CHAPTER 38: KILL THEM ALL

Eli

Brent and Sean have insisted on coming with me, and I'm glad about that. But I'm not glad that they seem to feel responsible for Kelly's disappearance since they'd left before they knew the girls were secure. They'd been so excited to see whether the rickety old van would make it all the way back to Mark's castle that they had just taken off driving and didn't wait for the other car to drive off.

I have told them multiple times that it isn't their fault, that Mark has insisted that Chris is a strong, capable warrior and whatever has happened, I'm sure he is doing everything he can do to keep Kelly and the girl, Heather, safe right now. Not to mention that Kelly can be a force to be reckoned with as well—I know I don't want to be on her bad side.

But I guess if I were in the same situation as Brent and Sean, I would blame myself too.

Eustace has also abandoned his attempt at restoring the old van to join us in the search as well. I imagine he feels the same way as Brent and Sean. Heather is one of his pack members, still a child, really, and she's missing, too.

They all seem to be doing better now that they are out with me looking for the girls and Chris. I'm sure it feels good to be taking some action to find them all.

My feelings, on the other hand, are completely torn and confused. I want my sister back now. But it kills me to leave Rose and my little Ethan behind, even though I know the other Alphas will protect them with their lives.

Ethan... what a beautiful name Rose had chosen for my boy.

Eustace is driving. We're in one of Mark's SUVs, and even though our mission is dead serious, he's got the shittiest grin on his face that I've ever seen.

"I... I ain't never in my life driven something as fine as this," he says, looking over to me.

I nod. This is a pretty nice, new vehicle, and everything's so rundown out at that old resort. I understand where he's coming from. "I'm sure Mark will let you drive several of his cars after we find Kelly and the others," I say.

"Ya think so?" he asks, taking his wide eyes off the road.

"Only if you watch the road," I say with a little laugh. It's not easy to laugh right now, but the look on Eustace's face is just comical. He's like a kid in a candy store.

I look in the side mirror at the caravan of warriors behind us. It's not a huge contingent because we needed to leave more than enough warriors behind to take care of all the threats at Mark's castle, but I have to say we look pretty impressive in our caravan driving down the road.

"Here she is," says Eustace, nodding forward at the bend in the road where we'd pulled over when we changed cars before, the night I was racing to get to Rose on time.

I still can't believe I'd made it just as my little son was born. He's the most beautiful thing I've ever seen in my life, next to Rose. My mind wanders for a few seconds to what happened after that... the blood on the floor, Rose not responding. 'No,' I tell myself. I can't let myself go there. Rose is healthy. The pups are all healthy. And they are all safe in Mark's fortress of a castle.

I snap out of it enough to use the mind-link to alert all the warriors in the cars behind us that we've reached the spot, and one by one, they pull over. Once all the engines are off, everything is so quiet and still. This is a highway, but it's rarely traveled, apparently. In the shadowy dusk we'd been in that evening, I hadn't given much thought to my surroundings. I'd had too many other things on my mind at the time.

A few warriors who are close friends of Kelly shift so they can look around for her scent. I stay in human form for now, looking around the desolate landscape. Something just doesn't seem right.

I feel a brush of air as Brent walks up beside me. "We saw nothing between here and the castle," he says.

I nod and reach into my mind for Tyler. His group is moving slower, checking out any side roads along the same route. 'Anything?' I ask him.

'Not yet,' he says. 'A few dirt roads have some signs of recent tire tracks, but we'd have to split up to check them all out.'

'Do it,' I say.

'Yes, Alpha,' he replies.

I know Tyler still blames himself for the Cora incident, but that wasn't his fault. He was happy that I'd made it back but was really upset with the deaths of Ben and Liam, not to mention Kelly's disappearance. When we get through all this, the other Alphas and I will make sure that everything is secure within our ranks. I know Tyler well and trust him, but I can tell that lately he's felt guilty.

I guess there's a lot of that going around these days.

'Alpha!' I hear one of my warriors in my head—Valda, one of Kelly's friends who is currently in wolf form. 'We have something over here, just off the road to the east.'

I run over and see Valda and some others gathered in a circle in the roadside brush. All of them have their noses fixed on something on the ground in front of them. I still haven't shifted yet, so I squat down to take a look at it.

"Auto glass," I say, picking up the piece.

'Yes, Alpha,' says Valda. 'Appears to be from a front headlamp.'

Brent comes jogging up behind me. When he's next to me, he

shakes his head. "That doesn't make any sense," he says. "I'm sure they'd started driving. There's no way they could have gotten into a wreck right here, where they hadn't even taken off yet."

'I'm not picking up her scent,' says Valda, confirming Brent's suspicions.

I nod. "This does look recent, but I don't see how it can have anything to do with her," I say. "And there's no other wreckage around."

Even though she's in wolf form, I can make out the frustrated and frightened expression on Valda's face.

"We'll find her," I say decisively. "Okay. Whatever happened, it happened somewhere between here and the castle. So, let's retrace our steps and help Tyler out. He's got some tire tracks to follow."

I sigh. I've been calling Kelly repeatedly in the mind-link, but still, there's no answer from her.

I refuse to believe that the worst has happened. I will find her.

ALASTOR

I'm positively salivating as I approach the territory of Alpha Mark. Such a minuscule task left for me to do, and then I'll rule the entire kingdom.

That idiot Gene is the perfect patsy. He's so stupid that he can't even tie his own shoes. This almost seems too easy, but I know I deserve this, so maybe that's why.

I look back at the other vehicles behind me; they contain some of the king's best warriors, and they've all agreed to be a part of something wonderful. The hardest part had been finding which ones I could trust to be on my side, and it turns out that wasn't a problem at all. Most of them had felt they had a shot at the kingdom themselves until those four despicable Alphas came along.

They're more than happy to help put an end to them.

What a stupid idea... to breed four Alphas with one woman. Ridiculous. But then, I expect nothing but stupidity from the soon-to-be ex-Alpha King. It's about the perfect karma that the woman bore four of the little brats, leaving the king so confused that he was more than easy to manipulate.

I see the top of the castle, which looks like some sort of rich man's mansion, appear above the horizon as we move closer. It doesn't even appear to be guarded…. They are such stupid Alphas. Their arrogance will pay off in my favor, I'm sure.

I instruct the vehicles to stop and the warriors to prepare to shift.

My simple task… is to kill four bratty pups, a woman, and four useless Alphas.

This is going to be fun.

CHAPTER 39: GIVING HER A CHANCE

"Yes, I know her," I say, looking at Retta and trying to figure out why in the world she, of all people, is here.

"Your parents sent me as a representative from our pack to help take care of you and the babies," she says, folding her hands in front of herself as she averts her eyes from me. "I know it's been a long time since we've seen one another. You look lovely–as always."

I stare at her, not sure how to reply. "I'm confused," I say, being completely honest. "Why would they choose you to come here? It's not as if you and I were ever friends."

Before the woman can even respond, Tristan says, "Do you want me to toss her out?"

It seems pretty clear to me that Tristan is on the defense, even more so than the other two Alphas that are here with me. Once again, I am missing Eli, which I don't like one bit.

"No," I tell him, using a calm voice. "I would like for her to explain to me why she's the one my parents chose. That's all."

Tristan sits back down, folding his arms, and I feel like I have my own personal bodyguard against bullies. It's too bad he wasn't in high school with me.

Retta won't look at me. "I've become a very good nurse and nanny over the last couple of years since we graduated from high school," she says. I've never heard her sound so humble before. Her voice is so quiet, it's almost like she doesn't think she's the most amazing person in the universe anymore.

"And what about your demeanor?" I ask her. "How do you explain that?"

Finally, she looks up at me, just briefly, catching my eyes before she drops hers again. "I can't really explain it, Miss Rose. I guess… the older I got, the more I realized that I wasn't anything special. I shouldn't have had the attitude I did in high school."

"You told me that you and Rose weren't friends because she was the Alpha's daughter, and you felt like she was unapproachable to you," Mark says. "But from what you're saying now, it seems like perhaps that's not quite the truth."

I almost laugh. "You said that?" I ask Retta. "Really, Retta?"

She shrugs. "It's true, though. I know it's hard to understand, but you were the Alpha's daughter, and I just felt like you were way too good for me, and if I were ever going to be able to measure up to you, I needed to pretend to be something I wasn't."

"A snob who told everyone that they weren't good enough to be friends with her, even if the person in question was the Alpha's daughter?" I clarify.

A low rumble emanates from the back of Tristan's throat. He wants to kill her, but I almost think it's comical. She's acting so differently than how she did in school, it's kind of funny to see her grovel a little bit.

"I'm very sorry, Miss Rose," she says. "I know I wasn't a good person back then, but after my mother passed away a few months ago, I've changed my ways quite a bit. I assure you, if you give me the chance, I will prove to you that I am a good nurse and a good nanny. I don't expect you to give me a chance to be your friend anytime soon, but eventually, I hope that you will see I am that as well."

I stare long and hard at the woman before me. I still see elements of the girl who used to make fun of me in the hallway at school or when she'd see me out and about in town. She had actually tried to tell Mark that I intimidated her? It is the biggest lie I've heard in a long time.

But she has a sincerity in her eyes at the moment that makes me want to give her a second chance. Perhaps it is the mother in me, but I am beginning to feel like there is a chance she means what she is saying.

Besides, there are plenty of other nurses from Mark's staff, people he knows and trusts, who are here with me. And I will be with my children at all times.

"Fine," I tell her. "I will give you a chance. But you've got to prove to me that you've changed."

I see a look of relief and joy wash over her face as she nods enthusiastically. "Yes, of course," she says.

Reece speaks up for the first time then. "Rose, we have plenty of healers and nurses in our packs we can send for that you can rest assured will be good for you and the babies. There's no need for you to settle for anything or anyone."

"I know," I tell him with a small smile. "And I appreciate that, I do. But… I think I'll let her try. It might be a nice lesson in humility."

He has hesitation written all over his face, but he nods at me. "Whatever you like, darlin'. But we will be busy with the war soon. I've just received word that this Alastor person has arrived in Mark's territory."

I nod at him. "You guys be careful and worry about yourselves. We'll be fine," I assure him. "I have a feeling now that all of the hardships are behind us now, that as soon as you defeat this guy, and Eli finds Kelly, everything will calm down, and we'll be able to happily raise our children."

He has a skeptical look on his face, but he nods and then leans down and kisses me.

The other two Alphas who are present kiss me as well, and then, the three of them rush out to assess the situation with their armies. I don't like it, them being gone, but the babies are all sleeping now.

"I think you should go get settled into your quarters," I tell Retta.

"Yes, of course, Miss Rose," she says. Her eyes travel over my children. "It's just... I think one of them has on a dirty diaper. May I check first?"

I take a deep breath and remind myself that's why she's here–to help with my children. "Sure," I tell her.

She quickly identifies that it's Ethan and changes his diaper quickly and without even waking him up. I am impressed. I haven't changed any of their diapers yet, but I have a feeling we would both be screaming now if it had been left to me.

Once my redheaded son is back in his bassinet, sleeping, Retta gives me a small smile and then leaves.

I'm not sure if I can trust her or not, but I won't be sleeping with one eye open–because I'm too tired for that.

CHAPTER 40: INTO BATTLE

Adam

We're still about twenty miles out from Alpha Mark's castle, although we entered into his territory quite a way back. Normally, I'd be pretty nervous entering into a powerful territory like this without an escort from the pack who belongs here, but times are very different now.

I'm no longer a Beta.

I'd worked my whole life to get my position, and for the past few years that hasn't been easy. Alpha King Gene's mind has been deteriorating for a while now, and I'd been proud of how well I'd kept the kingdom running smoothly while keeping the true nature of his competency out of the public eye.

I'd thought his Breeder idea was crazy at first, but the more I'd thought about it, the more sense it made. At least there would be someone else on the throne. And as it worked out, the four Alphas he'd chosen were more than competent, so at least that's one thing Gene got right.

In the long run, I guess hiding King Gene's deterioration had been a mistake. I should have been communicating with someone—anyone I could trust—as soon as the king's mind had faltered. Because now, I feel like this is all my fault. Everything that's happened or is happening now could have been prevented if only I'd told someone that the king was no longer fit for service.

So now, I'm going to prove my worth.

"I so don't like the look on your face," says Shelby.

I looked at her, my eyes glassy from the tears I'm fighting back. "You know me so well, my mate," I say. "I'm so sorry I've let you down."

"What the hell are you talking about?" she asks. "You've never let me down, Adam."

I shake my head and take things into the mind-link, sensing discomfort from the warriors in the front seat who have shifted positions. 'I'm not a Beta anymore,' I tell her. 'I can't provide for you the way you deserve to live.'

'Just what the fuck does that even mean?' she asks. 'Have I ever once asked to live in a castle or have a closet full of fancy clothes or anything else? I know we're never going back, and good riddance! Life was too stuffy there anyway. My home is with you, my mate, wherever we may be.'

She wraps her hand around mine and interlocks our fingers, squeezing tightly. 'I don't deserve you,' I say.

'Oh, for Goddess's sake, stop that,' she says. 'Of course you deserve me because I'm your fated mate, chosen by the Goddess herself, and nothing can come between us. Now, stop feeling sorry for yourself and get ready to fight these assholes.'

I laugh lightly as one of the tears escapes, and she leans over and wipes it away gently with her thumb. We don't need any more words between us.

I look forward and start to see the tops of Alpha Mark's castle against the clear blue sky. It's different from the Alpha King's home—more modern, like a contemporary mansion. But I don't have much time to admire it because there's something more pressing that demands my attention—a line of angry looking wolves in front of us.

Our caravan comes to a stop, and we all jump out, instantly shifting. I swear, I'll never get tired of watching the clothes rip off Shelby as she gracefully shifts into a regal wolf with shimmering chocolate fur. She's so beautiful in every form.

'Watch the front line,' she tells me in the mind-link in a teasing voice.

She knows exactly what I'm thinking. I nod lightly and look ahead at the snarling line of wolves who have just turned around. All I have to live for anymore is the beautiful wolf beside me. I really feel sorry for any wolf who tries to harm her. I'm so hyped up and ready for this, and I have the strongest Alphas in the kingdom backing me.

This is going to be fun.

~

KELLY

"Kelly?" Heather's voice calls out in the darkness. "Kelly, she's not back yet."

"I know," I say. "Try not to worry." I don't even sound convincing to myself. I have no way to tell time down here—wherever 'here' is—but by the rumblings of my stomach, I know it's been much longer than the girl, Kara, usually takes to come bring us food.

And it has me worried. I'd told her to try to get the key from the man who has it, whoever he is, and if she got herself hurt or killed, well, that's all on me now. From the limited time I've had to get to know her, I'm not even sure how old she is. But she's clearly still a child, and I shouldn't have asked her to perform such a dangerous task.

"She's been gone a while," says Heather. "You ain't thinkin' she's dead, are you?"

"No, no," I say quickly, although that very well may be the case. If it is, I'm not doing so well at protecting teenage girls right now, and chained up like this, I'm not sure what I can do for Heather if someone tries to hurt her, too.

"I'm hungry," she says.

"I am too, sweetie," I say.

I stand up, because all I can do to move my body around the way

I'm chained to the wall is stand up, then sit down again. And in the seated position, my hands are above my head. When standing, I can't quite reach my full height because the chains pull me down again. I really hope Kara has been able to get the key. Maybe it's just taking her a little more time to make it back here.

I can only stand up for so long, just enough to let the blood flow back to my hands, then I sit down again. But I stand back up the very next second as I hear the clank of metal from the turning lock.

Someone's here.

Heather and I both hold our breath, and the air stills around us as the door pushes open and light pours in. Every time that happens, we're blinded, and it's impossible to see.

"I'm back," says Kara.

We let out a collective relieved sigh as she approaches.

"I'm sorry I took so long," she says. "It took a while to get the key."

My heart leaps at the words—she'd gotten the key. "Did anyone see you?" I ask.

I still can't see her face, but I can tell that she's shaking her head as she unlocks my handcuff chains. It feels so good to be free. I stand to my full height and move my arms around, feeling the pins and needles in areas I hadn't even noticed were numb.

In seconds, she's unlocked Heather as well, and I run over to hug her—well, as well as I can run with the cramps in my legs. She cries into my shoulder, and I squeeze her tighter, pulling in Kara, who is now also crying. After a moment I back up, putting my fingers up to my lips. My eyes have adjusted now, so I know Heather can see me.

"We have to stay quiet," I whisper.

The girls nod, and I walk over toward the door. "What's down this hall?" I ask, taking a whiff. There's something familiar about the scent in the air, but I just can't quite place it.

Kara shakes her head. "Nothing but guards," she says, "and my room at the end."

"Your room," I say. "You live here?"

"Where is 'here'?" asks Heather.

Kara shrugs. "I've been here too long to remember," she says.

"We're underground, that I know. Whenever there's a prisoner down here, it's up to me to feed 'em."

"Who brings you the food?" I ask.

"The guards," she says. "There isn't much down here, so I mostly stay in my room. I'm not allowed by the upstairs door."

"How many guards?" I ask. The girls and I are in a weakened state, but I know I'll fight like hell to get out of here, no matter how big and burly these guards are.

"Four," she says. "And there are more upstairs. There's only the one way out."

"Well, we're going to find it," I say.

"You'd better eat first," says Kara. "I brought you all I had."

It'll take some time for me to plan out how to get past the guards, so she's right. We might as well build our strength up. I close the door, leaving enough of a crack to keep the light filtering in, then walk over to the girls.

The food tastes so good. This time, she's brought not only some of the same bread, but also some dried jerky that tastes like heaven. Being able to eat in a decent position, without my arms tied up all wrong, is a blessing of the Goddess herself. For a moment, I forget myself as we giggle lightly and enjoy the meager meal.

I don't even notice the sound of footsteps.

CHAPTER 41: THAT WOLF IS MINE

Tristan

I don't want to leave Rose's side. Not now. Not ever.

But it's clear to me that Alastor, whoever the fuck he is, is approaching Mark's castle in full force, and it's up to the three of us that are still here, as well as a large contingency from Eli's pack, to fight him off.

I'm not really scared of him at all. As a matter of fact, I know that he's severely outnumbered and essentially running to his death. But... we still have to fight.

So fight we will.

And when we are finished with him, Alastor will wish he'd never, ever heard of Rose, our pups, or any of the four of us.

The attack begins on the far left of our line where Reece and his wolves are positioned. I hear the other Alpha's voice through the mind-link telling me that the attacking forces are not just warriors from Gene's pack, but many of them are from neighboring packs as well.

That is a red flag in my head. Before, I assumed that we were just battling the few thousand warriors Gene would be able to scrape together after all of his recent battles, but if he had recruited warriors from neighboring packs, there's simply no way for us to know how many wolves were actually charging at us.

Before I can even say anything to anyone else, about how unsettling this is, the battle is in front of me, and I don't have a chance to do anything except for fight.

I am already in my wolf form, and I am larger than most of the wolves that are running at me, but I can see that many of them are elite warriors from other packs.

It seems quite clear to me that Gene truly has changed his mind about his initial plan to make the father of the first son Rose had into the Alpha King....

The line of warriors in front of me, from my own pack mostly, though a large section of Eli's troops have been given to me to command as well, leap forward, ready for the fray. It's difficult for me to stand back and wait, concentrating on giving them orders rather than fighting myself.

Right from the beginning, my fighters are sinking their teeth into the necks of the attacking wolves, and I want a piece of that, too.

I manage to keep my urges under control until I see a large wolf sauntering slowly forward through the tree line of the woods beyond the castle grounds. He's massive, and judging by the shade of gray his fur has turned, he's older, too, probably in his mid-to-late forties.

I want a piece of him. I have to think that this is the new Beta, that this is the guy that Gene has sent to attempt to wipe us out.

Right now, he's not doing anything but observing, probably giving orders through the mind-link, sort of like I am, but I really want to taste his blood, so I find myself moving my line forward, advancing over the ground more quickly than I normally would so that I can get a piece of him.

It takes a bit of time, maybe an hour, an hour and a half, but we drive them back enough that when I finally jump into the fray, I can justify going right after their leader.

He's not a true Beta, not born of a Beta, and therefore, he isn't capable of initiating a conversation with me as an Alpha, but I can talk to whomever I want to, so when I stare him down and say, 'What the fuck do you think you're doing? Attacking the rightful king of Black Rock?'

He only grins at me, refusing to answer with words, and as I cross the rest of the land between us, his response is to launch himself at me first.

I lower myself to the ground, my knees bent, and as he takes up off the ground, aiming for my head, I am easily able to dodge him.

He isn't deterred, though, as he gets up off of the ground and comes at me again, literally nipping at my heels. I spin around and face off against him, swiping at him and drawing first blood when I hit him in the upper shoulder.

'I've lost quite a few warriors,' I hear Reece say in my head, 'but I think we are finally starting to turn them back.'

I'm shocked to hear that. My warriors have done so well here in the center of the line.

Mark reports, 'Yes, I've lost quite a few as well, but I think we've been able to hold them off.'

'Uhm… what the hell?' I ask. 'Did he send all of his fiercest warriors to the flanks because the middle of the line is holding strong.'

'I don't know,' Reece says, 'but there were a lot of them, and they were huge.'

My mind can't focus on that right now as this massive wolf comes at me again. He comes at my neck this time. I slide down and but fall backward onto the ground, my spine landing on a rock. I don't have time to let the pain sink in. I kick up with my legs, catching him, and sending him flying up and over my head.

He slams into a tree, and I hear the cracking of his bones.

Somehow, he manages to push up off the ground, and I am ready to go at him again, but then, I hear a voice in my head.

'Wait, Alpha Tristan, please,' the male voice pleads with me.

I look up and see a group of wolves approaching at a high rate of speed from the same direction where the attack came, but I know immediately these are not enemies–these are friends.

'Wait?' I ask, confused.

'Yeah… I want a piece of him.'

I can't help but chuckle as the large gray wolf is clearly giving orders to his men that have broken and are falling back. He has no idea what's coming.

'All right, he's all yours,' I say in my head. 'Have fun… Adam.'

CHAPTER 42: PLAN B

Gᴇɴᴇ

Ah, the joy of it all. I don't know what in the world possessed me to think about giving up my royal title, especially after I'd worked so hard to obtain it, but now all is safe. I know that bastard Adam wasn't doing my bidding as he should have as my supposedly loyal Beta, but this new guy, Alastor... I'm positive that he'll do whatever I say.

And right now, he's off slaughtering those worthless Alphas and their spawn... and the Breeder. I have to dispose of that Breeder.

"It's ready for you, Your Majesty," says my servant, bowing his head as a good servant should.

I brush past him and push the useless peon out of my way.

Ah, my bath, perfectly drawn for me with just the right temperature of water and a soothing massage. I can smell the hint of lavender and the light suds look positively inviting, and—

"Servant!" I holler. I can't be bothered with thinking of his name right now. He's too insignificant for it to matter, anyway.

"Y-Yes, Your Majesty?" he says.

"What is the temperature of this bath?!" I bellow. "It's positively scalding! Are you trying to damage the royal toes?!"

"Y-Your Majesty," he says. "I... I apologize. I was mistaken about the speed at which you'd arrive for your bath. Normally, it needs some time to cool—"

"You are to prepare the bath to my standards when I command it!" I say. I can't believe this incompetent moron. No wonder he doesn't have a name. "Fix it, immediately!"

"Yes, Your Majesty," he says.

I stand here in my royal robe for what seems like hours before the idiot gets my bath right.

"I hope it is to your liking now, Your Majesty," he says.

I grunt and dip my toe in, and it's close enough. I just want this idiot out of here now so I can relax. "Dismissed!" I say loudly, and he bows and practically runs out of the room.

Good riddance! Now, I can truly relax. I disrobe and sink myself into the pure bliss of my royal bath, the bubbles gently tickling my skin while the massage jets ripple up and down my back.

'Your Majesty?'

A voice has invaded the privacy of my mind. It's an ally, not any of those miserable Alphas, so I guess I'll answer. 'What is it?' I ask.

'Your Majesty, we need to discuss the plans going forward regarding the pups.'

I so wish that her voice was more melodic and not the harsh, grading whine coming through my mind. Ah well, no matter. She's on my side, and she's my backup in case other plans fail. I don't think Alastor will fail, but people have been known to fail me lately, so I can't be too careful.

'Fine,' I say. 'I'm in my suite.'

She doesn't answer, but I assume that means she's on her way. That means I have a few more moments of bliss to myself before getting on with the unpleasant business of planning. Planning is always so hard.

Well, she is a beautiful woman, so this should all be pleasant, yet something about that voice coming out of that beautiful mouth makes me want to vomit.

"Your Majesty?"

Ah, there's the voice now. So much for an enjoyable bath experience. Well, that's the burden of being the Alpha King, I suppose. Alpha King—a title I worked for my whole life. Damn the male and female wolves who birthed me! They should have given me my birthright before I had to take it! I stand up to welcome her but can't reach my royal robe.

"Your Majesty, I—" Barbara bursts through the door and, upon seeing me, she's turning around with her face covering her hands. "Oh, for fuck's sake, can you please just hide that thing?"

I don't know what to think. Surely, it's an honor to behold the naked body of the great Alpha King! "We are wolves, my dear," I say, surprisingly calmly. She is a beauty, after all. Not too bad on the eyes herself. "There is no shame in the beauty of our natural state."

She mumbles something then, still looking away, something about keeping my natural state covered. I think that's what she says. I can't really tell.

"I shall not!" I bellow. I'm just so good at bellowing; sometimes I do it just for fun. "The body of your Alpha King is a beauty to behold!"

She finally turns around, though she seems to be confused as to where I'm standing. I see her eyes glaring straight at the wall, many feet higher than my stature. With a surprised look on her face, she finally looks down to meet my own eyes.

"I apologize, Your Majesty," she says. "I'm afraid I was simply shocked by your beauty." There's a softness in her voice now. But I have to be careful lest she get too excited by the presence of my stunning form.

"Never mind that," I say. "What have you to discuss that you interrupt my bath?"

"I'm sorry, Your Majesty," she says. "I just think we need to develop an alternate plan in case your new Beta falters."

I nod. "Yes, yes," I say. "I had been considering that myself. What is it that you have in mind?"

"Well," she says, and she puts a seductive look in her eye that sparkles in the light of the royal bathroom.

Maybe I should pull her into the bath along with me....

"I... I've been doing some research on psychology."

"Mixology?" I say. "Yes, I do love a good drink. Do you have any good new ones?"

"No," she says, inhaling and sucking in her lip. "Psychology, not mixology." She mumbles something again here, but I'm not quite sure what she says. "Psychology involves the mind. You have many interesting psychology books in your library on the subject."

"Ah," I say. I finally find my robe and throw it on, and Barbara seems to let out a breath. I guess I'm so handsome that I'm positively distracting. "Go on."

"Well," she says. "It seems possible that simply to remove the pups from their fathers and mother can go quite a way toward having the parents just give up in life."

"Is that so?" I say.

"Yes, it's so," she says. "Should Beta Alastor fail in his military operation, I think there is another way to make sure the Alphas never bother you again."

"Do tell," I say.

"Oh, but Your Majesty," she says. "I think it's best that I not reveal my plan right now. That way, you have plausible deniability."

"Paws what?" I ask. Sometimes I just can't understand this woman.

"Not paws," she says. "Plausible."

I just look at her because I have no idea what she's talking about.

She sighs. "It means that you can say you don't know about something, and it'll be believable, because you really don't know anything," she says.

"Do you think that's necessary that I not know anything?" I ask. "I'm the king, after all, and I should know everything. I don't think there's any point in not knowing something. Besides, I'm known around this kingdom for my brilliance! Do you really think that people will believe I don't know something?"

She looks at me, and her expression is blank and unreadable. But I swear there's a hint of a smile cracking onto her lips. I have no idea what's so funny.

Finally, she takes a deep breath. "In this case, Your Majesty," she says, "I do think that I should be discreet."

"You should be out on the street?" I ask. There she is, making no sense again. Why don't I have all people on my side who can express a coherent thought? That Alastor was the same way.

"No, Your Majesty." She seems to whisper the words, and if I didn't know better, I'd swear she is growing impatient with me. But I'm sure that could never be.

"Just trust me," she says. "I have a plan that will help you get rid of those Alphas, that Breeder, and the pups once and for all. But you have to trust me."

"Trust you?" I say. I think about it for a moment. Has she ever steered me wrong? I can't remember one way or another, so I don't think there's any harm in trusting her. "Okay," I say with a wave of my hand. "Do what you must."

Then, a wide smile grows across her face as she says, "Yes, Your Majesty. Right away." She bows lightly and then turns to walk away, that shitty grin still glued to her face.

I shrug and turn my attention back to my bath. The water is a tad cooler now, but it's still the way I like it. Whatever Barbara is up to, I'm sure it will work out fine.

I wonder what she's up to.

CHAPTER 43: MAYBE I CAN TRUST HER

The sounds of fighting from outside of the castle are unnerving. Even though the bulk of the fighting seems to be going on on the other side of where I am located with the babies, it makes me so nervous. I want to keep looking out the window.

"It'll be all right," Retta says, smiling at me as she lays Trisha back in her bassinet. "All of the babies are asleep with full bellies. You should rest, too."

I think she's probably right, but I can't sleep with all of that going on. "Maybe now would be a good time for me to use the breast pump?" I ask her. "I think it would be great for me to have some extra milk put aside, just in case my body decides to stop producing so much." As it was, I felt like a cow with its utters dragging the ground. My body definitely understood I had a lot of pups to feed.

"Sure, you could do that. Do you know how to use it?" she asks me.

I shake my head. "Actually, no. I have no idea. I figured I could just read the manual."

"Yeah, that's one way," she agrees with a nod. "Or I can help you."

"You know how to use a breast pump?" I know Retta doesn't have any kids. In fact, I'm pretty sure she hasn't found her mate. She used to date this popular boy in high school, Lance, but he ended up getting some other girl pregnant.

"Of course I know how to use a breast pump," she says with a little giggle. "I'm a midwife as well as a nanny." Her smile is comforting to me for some reason. I'm surprised by it. Normally, when Retta smiled at me back in high school, it would make my stomach turn over. Like I just knew she was ready to make fun of me.

She usually did....

"Okay," I say. "If you know how, I'm happy to learn from you."

"Let me go wash it. Even though it's brand new, you don't want any left-over residue from the factory getting into your milk."

That seems like a wise idea to me, so I let her go, resting my head back on the pillow as I pretend that the howls and snarls in the distance are nothing to be concerned about.

They do seem to be fading away, actually, and while I'm tempted to check in with one of the Alphas to see how the battle is going, the last thing I want is to be a distraction.

A few minutes later, Retta is back with the pump. She sits down next to me on the bed and says, "Let me show you how to put all of the pieces together."

It doesn't seem that complicated to me, and in a few minutes, everything is set up. I might've been embarrassed to whip my boobs out in front of another woman before I had the babies, but now, I feel like I am always on display for everyone anyway. So who cares if she sees my boobs?

I almost laugh, thinking of how awkward I had felt that first day when Shelby came into the bathroom with me.

But thinking of Shelby makes me sad....

"Are you all right?" Retta asks. "You can control the speed and suction here, with these buttons, if it hurts."

"No, it's not that." The machine was fine. My nipples were sore from all of those little chompers latching onto them, but the machine was soothing in a strange way. "I was just thinking about a friend of mine."

"Oh." She grows quiet, and as she gets up to straighten a few things over by the diaper changing station we have set up on one side of the room, she says, "I am sorry I was never a friend to you. Before. In high school."

"Yeah, you were always one of the popular kids." I am holding the cups on, but it's making me a little cold, so I pull a blanket up over myself as she continues.

"I was, but it didn't lead to the life I thought it would." I hear notes of sadness in her voice.

"What do you mean?" I ask her.

"I mean... dating Lance, trying to be so cool all of the time, it only led me to a dark place. When he left me for Irene... I thought I wanted to die. It really changed me, Rose. For the better. I realized then I could do a lot to help other people. So... I decided to make some changes, to start doing some good in this world."

I can't help but smile at her. Perhaps I had been wrong to judge her so quickly. "Well, you've definitely been helping me," I tell her.

Her smile is full of light and gratitude. "Thank you. When your parents asked me to come here and take care of you, I was surprised. But I was honored to be chosen."

I smile back at her. "I'm glad now that they chose you."

She nods and then asks, "By the way, have you spoken to them... recently?"

"No. They might've wanted you to come and look after us, but they haven't wanted to do so themselves." Saying so makes my heart heavy.

She gives me a half-smile of sympathy. "I'm sorry to hear that. I know your relationship with them was always complicated, but we could all tell how much they loved you."

My eyebrows furrow before I can even ask the question. "You could?"

Retta's eyes widen. "Uh, well... yeah. Of course. I mean... you're the only daughter of the Alpha and the Luna. Of course, they must've loved you–love you–a lot, right?"

"I never felt that way," I admit, wondering what it might've been about our relationship that made her think that.

"Well, I just mean that... as their daughter, you had certain privileges, you know? Servants... no after-school job, that kind of thing."

"Uhm, I had no servants. We only had a few, and those were only for my parents. And I had to work two jobs after school and on weekends to make up for my parents' irresponsible spending of pack money." I think back to the sewage treatment factory, and a shudder goes down my spine.

Retta is staring at me dumbfounded. "Really? None of us had any idea."

"Well... maybe you should've asked," I say with a shrug.

Slowly, she begins to nod. "Yeah. I should have. But I was just a dumb kid." She walks over to me and squeezes my hand. "I'm realizing I didn't know you at all, Rose. And I'm so sorry for that. It was me that was missing out."

I'm not sure what to think about Retta, whether we can ever be friends or not, but she is making me think I can trust her. And that's good because I have no idea where Kelly is, and I think Shelby is fighting in the battle that rages on outside.

Retta might be the only friend I have for a while, so I need to be able to trust her.

ALSO BY BELLA MOONDRAGON

One Night with the Billionaire

Shared by the Sexy Billionaire Twins

The Alpha King's Breeder series:

Bought by the Alpha: The Alpha King's Breeder Book 1

Loved by the Alpha: The Alpha King's Breeder Book 2

Lost by the Alpha: The Alpha King's Breeder Book 3

Luna of the Alpha: The Alpha King's Breeder Book 4

Legacy of the Alpha: The Alpha Kings's Breeder Book 5

Daughter of the Alpha: The Alpha King's Breeder Book 6

Descendants of the Alpha: The Alpha King's Breeder Book 7

Shadow of the Alpha: The Alpha King's Breeder Book 8

The Luna's Vampire Prince series:

The Culling

The Kingdom

The Conquered

Pregnant With Four Alphas' Babies

Chosen As the Breeder

Mated to Four Alphas

Threats Against the Breeder

At War for the Breeder

The Stolen Breeder

Four Alphas, Four Babies

Becoming the Luna Queen

Descendants of the Breeder (releases 9/1/2024)

Desired by the Devil series

Whispers of the Devil

Bantor of the Devil (coming soon)

The Mafia Kings series

Indebted to the Mafia King

Sign up for Bella's newsletter here.

Follow Bella on Facebook here.

www.ingramcontent.com/pod-product-compliance
Lightning Source LLC
Chambersburg PA
CBHW060636260626
47161CB00008B/2904